SYNAPSE

By

N. L. Silk

PublishAmerica
Baltimore

ISBN: 1-4241-9136-X
PUBLISHED BY PUBLISHAMERICA, LLLP
www.publishamerica.com
Baltimore

Printed in the United States of America

I dedicate this book to my parents.
They always believed in me.

Acknowledgments

First I want to thank Patrice who always encouraged me. She was there in the beginning. I will always be grateful for her patience through my many drafts. A very big thank you, Patrice, for all your gentle suggestions.

I also want to thank Judy who asked the question that started me writing down *Shadow Play*. She read the very first draft. I'm sorry it took so long for the final piece.

Table of Contents

Shadow Play

The Free Spirit

The spirit sees life everywhere. It delights in creating beauty and joy. The spirit is mysterious. It is the greatest of power and the gentlest of power. In the distillation of all of humanity's faiths and beliefs we must believe in the spirit—the wonder-worker: life.

CHAPTER 1

An excerpt from Dr. Geoffrey Allen's private journal, November 20th:

"...I've learned in my first human physiology class the definition of what is a synapse: the two neurons talking to one another. The thing that makes it go, think, sleep, breathe, and crap. In other words, that little electrical impulse that goes from one neuron to another along a neural pathway is what helps us function.

"The synaptic function can get screwed in two ways: by nature or synthetic. If it's nature, fatigue or a lack of oxygen can affect synaptic function. You know, not being as sharp. If it's synthetic, drugs, more drugs (and for grins) ordinary household toxic chemicals will work just as well. But, why am I writing all of this? Maybe because I'm questioning my self integrity.

"But we're humans and humans just don't know how to leave anything alone. Enters I-N, Inc. 3 years ago.

"They say to us, "Hey, guys! We got an idea! A plan! Let's see what would happen if we control the synaptic reflex through programming. You know, make someone do something that they wouldn't ordinarily do. We'll call this idea 'Synaptic Reflex Control'.

"'Great!' We say.

"Our university needed the funds and new research equipment (Maybe a cadaver or two). And, the boys and girls from I-N, Inc., needed the cheap labor.

"'You're doing a great job,' they tell us. 'Soon we'll be able to market SRC. We'll be able to help all the social deviates and socio-paths roaming freely out there. Just think, help empty psychiatric hospitals and prisons. The world will be such a wonderful place when that happens.'

"'Great!' We say.

'Then after a year-and-a-half, the boys and girls from I-N, Inc. come to us again. 'You know. We showed it to our people and buyers. They loved it. But there's a problem.'

"'Oh?' We say.

"'Yeah. How're we supposed to get a hold of the psychos and social deviates? They might be crazy, but they can spot a cop a mile away. And the ones in padded cells or behind bars—they know they have rights. So, we were thinking.' They pause here for effect. 'Let's continue to develop the SRT further. For cops— who volunteer, say for example—to catch those rejects and deviates. If we can use the SRC to manipulate a sick mind to be healthy, we can manipulate a healthy mind to be sick. Oops, we mean to think like a socio-path. You know, so the volunteering cop can blend in with the crowd and can apprehend the socio-path for help. Of course, you need to figure out a way to reverse the whole process so the volunteer can re-enter normal society. But, that shouldn't be a problem.'

"'But...' We (I) started to doubt our integrity. Screwing around with someone's brains was not my idea of a good time.

"'We'll donate more funding. We can rebuild a wing of your medical school. We'll increase your salary—substantially. You'll even be helping your government and your fellow human being.'

"'Our government.' (Uh-Oh).

"'They're one of our interested parties. Of course, they'd prefer to go through the private sector on this one. But, you know, things need to be changed around a little. Call your new project 'Synaptic Reflex Technology.' Develop it as a police simulation. We'll check back in a month or so.

"'Here's some money. Times are tough. Crime is really bad out there. What ever happened to the good old days of being able to stand outside of your front door—non-bullet proof, mind you—and not worry if you're going to get gunned down?'

"Am I doing the right thing? Are we doing the right thing? God, I only hope so."

An excerpt from Dr. Geoffrey Allen's private journal, May 3rd from the following year:

"I came across a copy of my wife's senior thesis. She used part of a quote from one of her favorite authors. I always liked the quote because of its message: The final distillation of all of our important faiths and values is that we have to believe in life. In doing so, we as human beings must have the spiritual capacity to keep zest in living."

CHAPTER 2

"And this," said Nicholas Colemore, Jr. as he unlocked the door, "is my humble dorm room."

"Which is your half?" asked his red- and long haired sister, Cecily. She very well knew that her brother's side of the room would be neat. She made a mental note on how meticulous his bed was made. Her brother's desk and overhead shelf was organized and—most likely—dust-free. Even the three pictures of family and friends were framed and hung in an organized fashion on his bulletin board.

"That," Nick said as he pointed to the right side of the room.

"Well, I'm impressed." Cecily went over to his desk and saw the framed picture of their family standing next to his blotter. The picture was taken to commemorate their summer vacation this year.

"I thought you would be. Now you've seen the whole campus."

"Not really. I haven't seen any really cute guys." Cecily turned around to face her brother.

"You're still in high school."

"So."

"How's Missy." Nick wanted to change the subject but he didn't mean to start a conversation about Missy.

"She's doing fine. Still hoping you'll change your mind about her."

"I still have her last 'going away' gift. Want a piece?"

"No, thanks. I'm trying to cut back on chocolate."

"When she goes to college next year, she'll find a real boyfriend. You're her friend, maybe you can help her. You know. First day in college. Fresh start."

"I'll try. But I hope it won't be like last semester. I'm done helping. Look where it got us."

"Tell me about it." He said as he ran his hand through his hair.

"Everything is calm at the shop." Cecily didn't want to talk about Missy. Why did Nick bring her up?

"Yeah? How's that?"

"Stan's on vacation."

"Has he made any new theats to Dad?" Nick was always concerned about his father's relationship with his business partner.

"Last week, Stan and Dad had a fight," answered Cecily. She sat down on Nick's bed.

As Nick pulled up his desk chair to sit down near his sister he said, "Tell me. Is Dad OK?"

"Oh, he'll be all right. Just a bruise from the screw driver."

"What!?! I should beat Stan into a bloody pulp!! Did Dad call the police and have the sonufabitch arrested!!"

"Dad didn't and won't call the police. Stan's his partner. Maybe Dad doesn't want Mid-City getting any bad publicity. Dad always says loyalty to the Colemore-Claye partnership is very important."

"Bullshit."

Nick thought about last year's 'Post-Christmas Party' for the Mid-City employees. It was usually held on December 26. As a tradition, each partner would take turns holding the party. Last year, the party was at the Colemore's home. There were about fifty people crammed into their modest home.

Nick was talking to Anthony Claye, Stan's oldest son.

"How's school?" Nick hated small talk, but he was one of the hosts. Nick could tell Anthony was as uncomfortable as he was.

"Fine. How's school with you?"

Nick didn't want to say only 'fine'. There had to be something else more to say. Nick gave a cursory shrug. "I'm going to be starting on a big project next fall so I'm getting as many classes as I can out of the way."

"That's great. I thought you were a doctor already." Anthony looked as if the spinach dip was more interesting than this conversation.

"I am. Ph.D. But right now I'm being funded so that I can dedicate the time on this project. Hopefully it'll only take the one year to complete."

"Then what'll you do?"

"I might continue with the university or I might get hired in a corporation."

"When I'm done with school I migh'…"

Jane Claye, Stan's wife, ran past them. She was sobbing. Stan was quickly behind her. The crowded living room parted like lake water would part from a speeding motor boat. Jane ran into the den to grab her coat and purse before she bolted out the door. Nick noticed the room became quiet enough to hear Stan and Jane yelling at each other outside.

Nick could feel a tightness in his stomach. He knew how much his parents had hoped that Stan would 'behave' himself during the party. He remembered that afternoon long before the guests arrived his mother said how much she disliked how verbally abusive Stan could be to the people around him.

Now, Nick mentally clicked off ten years that (and each year was progressively worse than the previous year) the Colemores had to tolerate Stan's verbal abuse. This year, Nick could add physical abuse to list.

"He-llo! With me? Any way," said Cecily.

Nick's mind came back to his room and Cecily. "Any way."

"Stan was in the back of the shop, late last Wednesday. Everyone was gone by then. Yelling and screaming about Hinckler being so incompetent. 'I have to stay late to correct this! I should fire Hinckler! That effing bla-bla-bla-bla!'"

Nick gave a small chuckle. "He's a very good mechanic and he can put up with Stan's crap. That's why he's Stan's assistant. And Stan always comes in early and stays late."

"Yeah, Stan's an idiot. The whole world knows that. This' what happened: Stan likes to trash someone's desk. He says he does it because he needs important paperwork to finish his projects at home. Last Wednesday it was Dad's desk. Stan called him up and started yelling at Dad. That's when Dad went to the shop and tried to calm him Stan down. And Stan said, 'Don't tell me what to do! Back here I'm in charge! You don't know nothing about this place!' And then Stan started to push Dad. And Stan said,' Come on do something, you stupid asshole! Can't fight?!' Then Dad said, 'Stan *I'm* not going to fight. Now just stop this. The way you're acting is just stupid. I'm sure what ever Hinckler did it was a simple mistake. I'm sure it can be corrected tomorrow. Why don't you just go home.' Then Stan said something else. I don't know. Dad wouldn't say what. And Stan picked up a screw driver on a bench and threw it at Dad. Dad, you know, put up his arms like this." Cecily demonstrated. "But it still got him on the forehead. Just a bruise. Didn't even break the skin."

"Anything else?" asked Nick.

Cecily continued. "A few days before that, when Stan came back from lunch, he came in the front office just clenching his teeth and saying 'I should kill that effing bastard! He's such an effing bastard!' He went out to lunch with Dad. Dad wanted to buy out Stan."

"'Bout time." Nick interrupted his sister.

Cecily agreed. "I mean let's face it. Stan is driving everyone crazy and Mid-City is losing business. At least Dad can buy him out and save what's left."

"Did he take it?" Nick was hoping that Stan would accept the offer. Ten years. Ten years of grief caused by Stan.

"Of course not! Stan can't afford to be bought out. How would he start his own company? Who would hire him?"

"Good point. Why doesn't Jane have him committed to a mental hospital. He does sound unstable. Remember last summer when Anthony, you, and I were working at the shop. Stan yelled all over the shop one day that he 'should kill her! It would be cheaper than a divorce!'?"

"I don't know why his wife won't. Or why the twins won't." After knowing Ben and Brian for so long, Cecily still referred to them as 'the twins.' "They are his family." She shook her head in disgust. "I don't know."

"I can see why Ben and Brian won't. But Anthony? Stupid. Useless." Nick said.

"That's everything." Cecily shrugged.

Nick's answer was also a shrug. Then he smiled. "I see you're taking Audra's suggestion and dressing a little better than last week when I came home." Nick said to change the subject.

"That little comment was no suggestion. And it still hurts."

"Awww. *Poor* baby." Nick couldn't help being sarcastic. Then he said, "I'm sorry."

"Apology accepted. But you're still an asshole for not coming to my defense.

"It's getting late. You want to go get something to eat? I know a great pizza place not far from here. Just about everyone from school goes there."

"Sounds good. Maybe then I'll get to see a few cute guys. You know, the ones who aren't your friends."

"Thanks." Nick replied just as sarcastically. Then in a more serious tone, "That way you won't get home too late."

Cecily jumped up. "I really don't care if I get home late. It's still summer for me. Classes don't begin until next week. It's still light out. And best of all, I don't have to be at work tomorrow."

"Wasn't referring to school or work. I was referring to not making Mom and Dad worry about you." Nick got up and returned his chair to its place. "Speaking of work, how's it going?" Nick said as he ushered his sister out of the room.

"I'm just doing little jobs." She shrugged. "It's art. You know, if it weren't for Uncle Steve, I wouldn't even have gotten that job."

They started down the empty hall. It was a Friday night. If there wasn't a game or another type of on-campus activity, most students preferred to leave for the weekend. After all, the university was out in the sticks and corn stalks in Illinois. Because Cecily, who was going to enter a college for the fine arts in Chicago the following year, wanted to come for a visit, Nick thought it would be best if he stayed on campus for the weekend. Nick felt that he had a lot of studying to do and the quiet would help him concentrate. If he did go home, he would lose studying time. All in all, he was glad Cecily had come to visit him. He liked to also have her company, But, it wasn't always like that.

When they were younger, they fought like typical siblings. It wasn't until they became teenagers that they started to be more civil to one another. (Teenagers. That was only a very short time ago.) Nick learned to appreciate Cecily's "free-spirit". In turn, Cecily learned to accept Nick's meticulous, analytical reasoning. In other words, each one learned to like what the other one lacked.

"Connections help," Nick answered.

"They don't hurt," said Cecily as she walked by her brother's side.

CHAPTER 3

Audra Kramer had been a technician for the school's research lab at the university for the past three years. When she first met Nick, she enjoyed walking him through the simulator for the SRT monitoring- and testing rooms. Walking Nick through wasn't like walking the "administrators" or various "patrons of the sciences." Their walk-throughs were as easy and second nature to her as breathing. Quite frankly, when it came to showing non-personnel the rooms, she was almost bored. Yet, she noticed something odd when she had to deal with other people that made her uncomfortable. Ever since she was seventeen (and when she had her braces off and her acne cleared up), men (and a few women) sometimes developed the incredible urge to ask her out.

She always had a vague idea that she was OK looking. She had shoulder-length, brownish-red hair that she kept either in a bun or a ponytail for work. She had hazel eyes. Her face had just enough freckles to annoy her. All these features she felt were plain. However, what she thought and what others thought were different. When she was giving tours of the rooms, men looked as if they were trying their best to maintain their composure and not end up slobbering all over themselves like rabid Pavlovian dogs.

When she first met Nick, she noticed that his whole face lit up. His face said, "I want to ask you out!" Instead, he quickly diverted his eyes and cleared his throat nervously after they shook hands. To her, Nick acted like an awkward 14 year old during that first moment.

Then Nick turned his focus on the task at hand and he was all business. Yes, Audra liked Nick *because* of his shyness. It was a month on a Thursday before Nick got the courage to ask her out for a movie and dinner at one of the better local pub/restaurants.

She discovered that aside from excelling in science they both liked football. They liked the same kind of movies and food. They had the same kind of humor. They even came from similar family backgrounds of close-knit families and both parents were still married to one another.

Audra learned that Nick had a pet project. Nick was writing a virtual reality game and that he was far from having it completed. He told her that the project was his way of diverting hid mind from his other daily stresses. What impressed Audra the most was that Nick was so self-effacing: he was not a braggart.

Audra's first assessment of him was right—Nick was more than a 23 year old wunderkind.

Now they were doing the first of what was going to be many tests in their newly built SRT laboratory.

"OK, Nick. I'll be over here at my computer. Would you like to do any setting up?" Audra said.

"No, thanks. Just make sure you can see and hear everything that's going on with me when I'm in that," he pointed his thumb towards the other room, "thing." They looked at the machine through the window. The top half of the SRT unit was open and to Nick it looked like it wanted to swallow him whole.

Nick walked over to the middle computer and sat down to type on the keyboard.

"Second thought, I'm just making sure that everything's monitored and recorded. The entire test." Then he got up and sat in front of the computer to the far left. "I'm making sure the first program is OK."

"Don't make any changes. Not a good idea." Audra asked.

"Don't worry." Nick replied smiling.

Audra definitely wasn't a risk taker and there were protocols that needed to be followed with any changes or revisions.

When Nick was done reviewing all the routines and protocols, he got up and went through the swinging hospital-sized door and into the smaller white room where the machine stood. He went over to the long white cylinder machine and looked at the panel by the headrest to make his final inspection.

'Some day we won't have to use a machine like this for SRTs. We might not even have to bother with being hooked up like we're getting an elaborate EKG or EEG. Having stuff stuck on my arm, chest, and head doesn't appeal to me. Come to think of it. I really don't look forward being in a place that reminds me of a coffin,' Nick thought as he finished.

"I really hate this thing." He said it out loud so that Audra could hear him. He passed his hand by the air ducts from the cooling system by the headrest. He felt cool gentle air. Good. The air ducts would be working while he was testing.

"I can give you medication that Geoffrey ordered to relax you if you want it."

"Thanks for the reassurance. I don't think it will help, but I'll take them anyway." As Nick walked away from the machine and into the control room, he stopped and looked at Audra. "Why is everything white in here? Even the upholstery inside of the machine is white.

"Why not? Maybe it's for aesthetics. Decor," Audra said as she made an attempt at jollity.

"Yeah, right. You want to me to go change now?"

"Good idea."

Nick walked out of the control room and made an immediate right. There were locker rooms: one for women and one for men. He walked through the door with the picture that was to indicate the men's locker room. He went to the cabinet where green hospital clothes and disposable slippers were kept before he went to his own locker. When he was done changing from the campus uniform of well-worn jeans, university sweatshirt, socks, and old sneakers, he checked his right wrist to make sure he wasn't wearing his watch. The workings of watches did strange things to the finely tuned electronics of the SRT. The tan line of his wrist was a definite indication that he had remembered to remove his watch.

Nick closed and locked the orange colored door of his locker with the brass and plastic key that was kept in the keyhole until it was removed. He looked at the long row of lockers. Some of the keys were still in their keyholes. Nick allowed his mind to concentrate on the unused lockers as a temporary diversion. He was becoming nervous about the first test.

Why did he volunteer? Money? Remember who's paying: the public sector. He could always teach undergrads. The words 'job security' came forward the quickest in his mind after the very small figure on the upper right-hand side of his pay check appeared. (Most of the amount will cover his tuition and a few beers and pizzas.) The words 'signed contract' and 'knowing exactly'—down to the last comma and period—what will be done during the testing process came to mind next. Everything was in the contract, even the wording about what was going to go in was going to be taken out. Crap... Was all this going to be worth it? The risk? Or was this some very twisted version of being curious enough to 'stay to the very end of the movie.' What if... Think about all the laurels, the future funding, job security...

When he turned and headed for the control room to begin the SRT, Nick noticed his legs were a little shaky. This SRT, the first full-run test that the university's SRT research team and their volunteers were to do represented that there were no more fun and safe video games. This first full SRT was going to be real (if it succeeded). What if he came out of it with an IQ of oatmeal? If he walked away as bright as a small pen light? Then what? But. But, if it did work, the way psychiatric hospitals and prisons were run today would change dramatically if the SRT was successful. Think about that for a while.

Nick entered the control room and accepted a little paper cup with a single tablet that Audra offered him. Nick raised the little cup in a 'cheers' salute, emptied it and then exchanged it for another cup that held water. Audra threw away the little cups when Nick was done.

She then handed him another cup of water and another cup containing three different pills from the crash cart.

"Mud in your eye." Nick said as he unceremoniously emptied both cups. He hoped the tranquilizer would take effect very quickly.

"Now for the fun part," Audra said.

"I can't wait," he replied as he headed from the other room. "When will Geoffrey be here?"

"In about 15 minutes."

"Try to go easy on the goop." Nick said.

"Hee-hee-hee," Audra said smiling. "It's my only pleasure around here to see how uncomfortable I can make you."

"Great."

"Iiiiit's gooop time!"

Nick had to smile at her parody of Ed McMahon saying 'Heeeere's Johnny!' Some nights, Nick would go over to Audra's apartment and watch her collection of 'Tonight Show' DVDs with her. Her parents had taped some of the shows when their favorite stars were on and they still had the original videos. Now Audra had a very fine collection. It wasn't just watching old 'Tonight Show' episodes that he enjoyed. After all, Audra happened to be with him when he watched the shows.

CHAPTER 4

"Hi, how are you doing in there. Can you hear me OK, Nick?" asked Dr. Geoffrey Allen through his speaker.

Nick's mind said, "Feel great. Why are you screaming? Must be the leads. Great drugs."

The monitors in the control room read *Feel great. Why are you screaming? Must be the leads. Great drugs.*

Audra looked at the lower portion of her monitor. "He's flying," she commented with a light grin.

The doctor looked at the technician and then turned back to his monitor. "OK, Nick. This is for everything. Let's see what this all can do. To the future."

To the future. Nick answered.

"Begin the 'Police Simulation Program,'" said Dr. Allen.

"Starting it now," said Audra as her fingers clicked against the keyboard.

Click. Click. Click-click-click. Click-click.

Nick could hear the computer keys clicking in the distance.

Hey, Audra! I can hear you typing.

Click. Click-click-click-click. Click-click. Click, click. Police Simulation Program. Click. Click. Click-click-click-. Click-click.

The top half of the monitors showed

WHITE

BLACK

BLACK

GRAY

SYNAPTIC REFLEX TEST

PROTOTYPE

PROGRAM ONE

Police Simulation Program

The very bottom of each monitor showed the data of the program, Nick's vital signs including all brain function, and the SRT program's interpretation of Nick's emotions.

Yet, Nick saw, or at least his mind thought it saw

WHITE

BLACK

BLACK

GRAY

SYNAPTIC REFLEX TEST
PROTOTYPE
PROGRAM ONE

Police Simulation Program

Click-click. Click. Click-click-click.

Dr. Geoffrey Allen, a man in his late thirties, sat back to watch his monitor and see Nick's initial patterns that his brain made. As he continued watching, he fished through his lab coat pocket for his recorder and set it next to his computer. Everything appeared normal to the doctor.

So far, Nick was reacting and responding along with the program with Audra's inputted data. No deviations (or rather memories) from the SRT Program. There would be a problem then. If Nick fell into a memory, he would veer off the Program. The only way Nick could be placed back into the computer program is if Audra keyed in the necessary data. For Nick, that would be painful. If Audra made a mistake—a simple typo—or pulled him back into the SRT Program too early or quickly from the memory, Nick might end up a blubbering idiot.

Dr. Allen was glad he made the correct choice in his career. He chose research over a conventional medical practice. He preferred that his assistants called him by his first name when they were working on the project. However, that was where his being unconventional ended. When in public or dealing with the public, he preferred to be called 'Dr. Allen.' To him, curing people was not (what was the correct word to his feelings?)...didn't give him that same sense of accomplishment as research.

When he was 6 years old, there was a huge tree in the backyard. He would dig a hole by that tree, hoping that he would find buried treasure. He really believed he would find treasure if he dug deep enough. One day he did. Fake coins and rhinestones that were left there by his mother for him to find. It was like that: a sense of the thrill of discovery like that little boy who spent his days digging in the backyard pretending to find buried treasure and then really finding something. Now as a grown man, research was the only way to feel that same kind of thrill he had felt as that little boy digging by the big tree in his backyard. Dr. Allen was glad that he still had that little boy tucked away inside himself.

He stopped himself from letting his daydreaming run wild and concentrated on the situation at hand when he realized that Nick was beginning the Program.

The monitors showed

SYNAPTIC REFLEX TEST
PROTOTYPE
PROGRAM ONE

The monitor flickered again.
Then the monitor showed
 Police Simulation Program
 Ready to Continue

While the bottom right of the monitors showed

Ready to Continue

Nick's mind saw

SYNAPTIC REFLEX TEST
PROTOTYPE
PROGRAM ONE

Police Simulation Program
Ready to Continue

Geoffrey saw images flash on his monitor. The doctor was seeing what Nick and Audra were seeing.

GRAY
GRAY

Nick carefully walked through the shadow-casted halls. He gripped his gun to reassure himself. Inside the machine, Nick's left hand seemed to grip an imaginary gun. He looked at the shadows play against the walls. He quickly aimed to shoot. Then stopped. He thought he saw someone. It was only the moonlight through the trees outside of the opposite window. The light and shadows fell against a picture of a teen-aged girl on the wall. The effect momentarily gave the picture animation and from the corner of his eye, it seemed that another person was with him in the hall.

Click-click. Click-click-click-click.

Hey, Audra! I hear you typing again, I'm glad I'm not alone flashed the message on the monitors.

Nick thought while the monitors read, *Teen-aged girl. My sister. We used to fight when we were kids. Light.*

Something slammed through Nick's mind before he saw

BLACK
BLACK
GRAY

As Audra keyed in the data, the monitors showed

BLACK
BLACK
GRAY

The doctor made a note in Nick's chart about the personal memory (a deviation) during Synaptic Reflex Testing.

The monitors showed

MEMORY

Then the following scene formed on the monitors:

Nick and his sister were sitting on the concrete and granite steps of the fine arts building where Cecily hoped to attend school. It was a sunny day with a slight breeze that trailed down the busy city street. Students carrying huge book bags or art portfolios scrambled in and out of the huge double doors of the building.

"I sometimes feel Dad is still upset with me," said Nick.

A college student dropped his book bag at the bottom of the step and swung his guitar case around from his back, took it off and opened it to begin playing. A few strums of tuning joined Nick and Cecily's conversation. The college student began to play.

"To be honest, he would rather see you taking over the shop. But, he said it's OK doing what you're doing," answered Cecily.

"Truck and car engine parts never enthused me."

"I know."

A helicopter passed over them. Nick momentarily looked up and then back at the guitar player, who was now joined by a young woman and her saxophone.

Nick and Cecily stopped talking for a while and listened to the two musicians play a jazz song while they watched students and visitors pass by them during the late Spring day. They both loved people watching.

"Why did you choose to go into physics?" his sister finally asked.

Nick shrugged his shoulders, then leaned back against the step above him. "Physics with bio-engineering," he corrected. "Because I'm good at it. It's that the usual reason? I don't really want to take over Dad's business. Not with Stan around and I really don't like Stan's sons enough to want to be their partners. But then again, I could ask you why you're going to art school and not taking over the business too."

A sound of another helicopter flew over them. An ambulance

screeched around a corner at Nick's left. A man in an old army coat took out his guitar and started to play a few strings with the first two musicians.

"Because I'm good at art. I'm an artist." Then she said as she stood up to model her multi-colored and patterned outfit, "Where else can I get away with dressing the way I want to? I made it myself." Before she sat down she turned around so her brother could get the whole affect.

"Yep. You did. You blend in with the crowd. In fact all you artsy-fartsy students look like Picasso threw up on you." said Nick as he smiled.

Cecily's rebuttal was giving her brother a quick gesture (the American high sign for human propagation) while she said,

"Bite me." Then she said, "Maybe I won't visit you at *your* school in the fall."

"I'm sorry. I overstepped?"

"Big time," replied Cecily.

The monitors showed

END OF MEMORY

Nick saw

BLACK
BLACK
GRAY

While he heard

Click. Click-click. Click, click. Click-click-click.

"He's back in the Program," Audra said.

Dr. Allen spoke into his recorder that was pressed up against his mouth. When he got back to his office later today, he would replay everything. He clicked the recorder off and placed it next to his keyboard. He wrote more notes in Nick's chart.

Nick walked into the moonlit living room. He heard heavy boots clumkmp on the tiling by the entrance way. Nick saw the shadow dance in the room. He clicked his gun to be ready to fire in the direction of the sound.

It came again, the slamming sensation. Yet, this time the pain didn't feel like it was shuddering through his brain: it was much worse.

"Geoffrey, there's something wrong," Audra said as she tried to keep up with the speed of the data with her inputting. "I don't know how to explain this. Look!" Audra didn't have to worry— the doctor was watching in amazement. "It looks like the temporal lobe and hippocampus are trying to take over. The patterns aren't corresponding to the SRT Program."

Dr. Allen sat closer to his monitor.

They both continued to watch in horror as the data on the screens seemed to fight for attention. It was as if someone were trying to watch two different TV channels, one an accessible channel and the other inaccessible, by switching back and forth between the two stations to the point where one TV program seemed to be an overlay of the other.

Audra's fingers were trying to keep up with the data.

Crap. Crap. Crap. "Don't bring him up yet. At this point, we might lose him. Just stay with him," responded the doctor. He tried to keep himself from panicking. At the same time he wondered what they were discovering. He hoped Nick was going to be all right. Integrity.

"I'm trying." Audra was typing too fast to really allow herself to feel the full extent of her fright for Nick.

Click. Click-click-click-click. Click. Click. Click. Click-click-click-click. Click-click.

The flickering scenes on the monitors stopped to
   show that
      the lights came back on in the living room.
      And then there was a flicker.

Nick saw the remains of a blood and gore splattered body slumped against a wall.

"I think we got him…" Audra muttered something under her breath. "No. Sorry."

The monitors flickered off again and showed

BLACK
GRAY

Then they showed

SRT PROGRAM ONE

But then showed

static

and then

MEMORY

"What the HELL IS GOING ON!?! This is not supposed to happen!" Dr. Allen saw the entire project be removed from his control by the University's administrators.

"I don't know."

static

Then. Then it was as if a piece someone else's memory was trying to superimpose itself onto Nick's own memory. And. Now it looked as if... Nick's mind was fighting over... The

SRT program was fighting to come through the first phantom memory.

Audra was really worried about Nick. She could feel a headache trying to pulse to her temples.

Pictures and words flashed on their monitors.

Then their monitors showed

* * *

Nick's eyes were closed but he knew that it was light out. The sunshine tried to strain through his lids. Nick felt warm.

Something was making his bare arms and neck itch. He smelled clean straw and the odors of horses. He thought he was back at camp. He opened his eyes and looked around.

He was in a barn and he was laying in a stall on fresh straw and an old horse blanket. A pitch fork was propped against one side of the stall. Dusty light strained through the dirty windows.

Now he sat up to get a better look. Then something occurred to him. Ma and Pa would be mad at him when he got home. He was most surely going to get a whipping.

How do I know that? I don't call my parents 'Ma and Pa'."

Nick stood up.

Everything is so big… Why? Then he understood who he was. *I'm a little kid.*

He heard voices. He knew that those voices belonged to his two bosses.

Who were they? Oh, yeah. Mr. Kurtz and Mr. Graham. He's nice, Mr. Kurtz is. He works a lot and gets dirty like Pa. He gives me candy sticks sometimes. He always tells me that he bought one too many f'r his three girls.

Mr. Graham boxes m' ears sometimes. Mr. Graham thinks 'M good f'r nuthn'. Not so. 'M never goin' t' wear them sissy, city clothes that h' wear.

Nick crouched down and crawled to be closer to the voices. He was afraid that if Mr. Graham caught him, he would be beaten. Nick quickly stopped crawling when he heard gun shots. He sprawled face down on the straw-covered dirt floor. His eyes were closed tightly, he covered his head with his arms. He clamped his mouth in the hope that he wouldn't make a sound.

He shuddered at each fire of the gun. Then it was quiet. Nick opened his eyes and saw a spider scurry passed his face.

And…

"I think I can get him. His responses are slow enough." Audra said.

"OK. Grab him… Here!" Geoffrey ordered.

"Doing it now." While Audra typed, she had one thought of relief, 'It's over.'

SYNAPTIC REFLEX TEST

PROTOTYPE

PROGRAM ONE

End of Police Simulation Program
Click. Click-click. Click-click-click.

The monitors showed

BLACK
GRAY
GRAY
WHITE

Nick saw

BLACK
GRAY

GRAY
WHITE

before he fell into a very deep sleep.

When he woke up, he saw the lid of the machine open. He felt his left arm and head. He was no longer hooked up, but he would need a good shower because of the gel and the sweat he had built up while he was under the test. Nick heard movement in the little room before he saw Audra peer over the edge of the machine.

"How're feeling?" she asked with a forced smile.

"Like crap. My head really hurts. A lot." It bothered him that Audra was trying not to look worried. Why was she worried?

"I wish I could give you something more. But I don't think Geoffrey really can't prescribe something else. One of the little pills was supposed to prevent you from getting headaches."

"Well, take a wild guess what didn't work," he said as he tried to sit up. The throbbing continued to get worse with the exertion. He grimaced from the pain the headache was causing him. He hated to show that he was in pain.

"Easy, Nick," said Geoffrey. He suddenly appeared in the room and by Nick's side.

"Just show me where the floor is and I'll be fine." The room suddenly lurched into a casual somersault.

43

CHAPTER 5

It was night and Dr. Allen Geoffrey in his office upstairs from the research lab reviewing the CD from Nick's test. He reached for his recorder while continuing to watch the data and final scene scroll on his monitor. He brought the recorder to his mouth and began to speak into it.

"I think we have proof of innate memories. I never believed in collective memories or ancestral memories; however, from today's test all the data shows that innate memories may be real.

It was always speculation that our ancestors had the ability to retain past- or collective memories. Like birds do. And as we humans developed, we lost the ability to retain past- or collective memories." He smiled to himself as he sat back and clicked the recorder off.

In a dorm room on campus, Nick finally got to sleep after a lot of tossing and turning interrupted by trying to form patterns from the cracks and water stains above his bed. it took most of the afternoon and into early evening for the thudding pain in his head to finally subside…

SRT

        I have

again   tomorrow.

* * *

He was standing in a huge building with walls made with wooden planks and a dirt floor. He could see that the sun was straining to come through the dusty windows.

Five wagons and two coaches in various stages of completion occupied most of the floor space. Nick also saw the equipment that was for heavy repairing of these wagons and coaches.

A man in dirty and sweat-stained work clothes was bent over a broken wheel that he was repairing by himself. Nick wanted to go to the man in the dirty clothes and warn him about something.

"What do I need to tell him?" Nick asked himself.

Movement caught the corner of Nick's left eye. He looked to see a silhouette of a big man in the wide doorway. Nick couldn't see any other feature: the bright sunlight shielded the man.

"James Kurtz. You son-ufa-whore!" The man in the doorway bellowed as he came into the building. He was dressed in a dark brown suit and bowler. Nick could see that he had his right hand hidden in his topcoat. Nick remembered why the big man's hand was hidden. As the big man walked to James Kurtz, he took his hand out of his coat. Nick saw that the man was holding a gun and was aiming it at James Kurtz.

"No. Don't shoot him." The words Nick said came out as some of kind of obscured whisper, as if his mouth were clogged.

James Kurtz stopped working as he saw the gun and stood up. "Harold. No."

"You ruined this place. You made me go bankrupt!" Yelled Harold.

"Harold," James put up his hands, palms out. "Please, let's talk. I can pay you back. Every last penny."

This time the words came out as Nicked yelled, "Stop! No!" as he heard Harold's gun click. This time the words came very clear and loud. The two men ignored Nick.

The familiar shattering sound went through James Kurtz's body. His blood splattered against the wagon wheel that James was working on and onto the dirt floor. Nick noticed how the blood tried to blend into the hard packed floor.

"No!" Nick yelled again. He tried to run to what was once James Kurtz but he couldn't move.

Nick smelled the musky odors of horses and the acrid scent of smelted iron mixed with gun smoke. He thought he smelled blood and the eyes of James Kurtz.

The eyes.

Kurtz's eyes were staring at him, pleading for help and...

Nick tried to scream himself awake. When he stopped screaming, he found that he was awake and sitting upright in bed. He was also sweating.

"Hey, are you alright?" his roommate, Peter Young, groggily asked. Peter was propped up on his left elbow.

"It was nothn'. Bad dream, Pete. Go back to sleep."

Peter complied by rolling onto his back and immediately began to snore.

Once again, Nick spent an hour-and-a-half staring at the cracked and water stained ceiling over his bed trying to find logical patterns. He also thought about what he would be doing tomorrow. He finally got back to a very fitful and shallow sleep. He had a feeling that by morning he wouldn't want to get up, but would rather stay in bed. Unlike the majority of collegians, he knew he couldn't and wouldn't skip his morning class. Besides, he had to do another run through with the SRT machine at 1:00 tomorrow.

CHAPTER 6

"You look like hell! What happened to you!?"

"Good morning to you too, Audra. Bad night." Nick said as he shuffled into the room and took a long swig of his extra large black coffee.

"No kiddin'. Do you want to call it off?"

Nick took two beats to answer. "No."

"Well, then shall we?" She gestured towards the SRT room. Nick tried to muffle a yawn. He really wanted to go to sleep in his own bed. But, he supposed that having to sleep under medication in the SRT machine was just as good an alternative. Dreams could wait. He hoped that last night's nightmare was just his anxiety about today's test. Then again, if last night was what could be expected, then he could definitely wait to dream. He knew one or two college students made it a habit of catching a few "zzzs" in class or in the campus library.

"Hi, Nick," Geoffrey said as he entered the monitoring room.

Nick raised his right hand in a 'hello' gesture as he tried to muffle another yawn.

"Bad night. Very bad night." Nick said between the yawn.

"You want to talk about it?" asked the doctor.

"I dreamt that I was reliving what happened to me in the SRT machine yesterday. Sort of. I think. But, last night (yawn) it was worse." Nick watched Geoffrey write some notes in his chart. Geoffrey's brow was furrowed.

"'Sorry. Policy that I have to note everything. In the name of research." Geoffrey said.

Audra handed Nick a cup of pills.

"To research." Nick raised the cup of pills in a 'cheers' gesture.

"Do you want to go through with this today? If you don't feel up to it we could…"

"Might as well." Nick slammed back the cup of pills and then chased it with the cup of water that Audra handed him.

SYNAPTIC REFLEX TEST
PROTOTYPE
PROGRAM TWO

Police Simulation Program

Nick knew it was in the early morning hours when he walked to the abandon building on the water front. The rusted chain and lock was broken and clanked against the weather beaten and rusted fence. As Nick went through the gate, he stepped on a rusted metal sign. He looked down. Nick's right foot covered part of a peeling rust word:

"Engine."

Engine.
GRAY
GRAY

Geoffrey was sitting back in his chair talking into his recorder when he saw the scene on his monitor flash off and on quickly. Much quicker than yesterday. He stopped the recorder and sat forward.

The flashing stopped. His monitor now read

MEMORY

"We're losing him. I hope we're not repeating this like yesterday." Audra said. She could have sworn she checked every last letter of the program this morning.

"Catch him. And then erase it. You're right. It's just like that part of the yesterday's test. All the data is going wild—again. Look at all the output! No wait. Stay with him and let the SRT run. Can you manipulate the memory instead? Let's not push or hurt him." So much for today's test. Geoffrey was torn between what the funding corporation wanted and what his conscience wanted. Money or ethics, which would win? I-N, Inc. or his integrity? Would he find buried treasure in the hole by the tree or not?

"Pearson won't like this. He wanted to see results—good results. Personally, I care more about Nick than for the people paying us to do this."

"I agree. Screw Pearson."

Click-click-click. Click. Click. Click.

BLACK
GRAY

Their monitors saw

Engine

Nick thought "Engine."

GRAY
GRAY

Nick assumed that he was inside the building. Heavy machinery and dirty work benches seemed to crowd around him.

A man in a gray business suit sat at a desk by a double door doing paperwork. Nick stood about 20 - 25 feet from the man behind the desk.

Nick tried to walk to him but he couldn't move his feet. He was about to call out to the man in the gray suit when another man in a brown business suit walked through the double doors and stood directly in front of the man behind the desk. His right hand was concealed in his suit jacket.

The man in the gray suit stopped working and looked up.

"Kevin! Good morning! How are ya'?" I'll be ready to go in a minute." He said cheerfully. "Too bad the wives can't go."

GRAY

GRAY

Then the monitors showed a silvered blip in the center of each screen followed by static.

"What happened to visual and audio?!" Geoffrey really didn't like the way this SRT was turning out.

Audra was just as puzzled. All three monitors also then went blank. The audio seemed to go in and out with a fuzzy, muffled sound. It quickly occurred to her with a blush what had happened. "I think the optical and audio leads came loose."

"Son-ufabitch," Geoffrey muttered under his breath. He was really angry. And, tomorrow he had to have a report in to Pearson. By Monday, Pearson had to take that report to the administrators of the University and I-N for a presentation. The big fish gobble up the little fish. And we all know what rolls down hill. "Is everything still being recorded?"

"Yes. Maybe we can edit the whole thing together."

"How do you suppose you're going to do that without optical?"

Audra just gave him a smug smile to try to cover her embarrassing error with the leads. "It's amazing what technology can do. There's still the back-up optical and audio leads for the computer. If they're still attached to him, the computer is storing all that in a separate program." She continued to enter data from her keyboard as she craned her head to read the print out. She definitely preferred her monitor. At least there wasn't such a huge time lapse to get output. Her printer was annoyingly slow.

"KEVIN SHOOTING HIS PARTNER... THREE MORE TIMES... ALL THE BLOOD... GORE... HIS NECK... I THINK I SEE

BONE... ALL THE BLOOD..."

Geoffrey turned to read his printout:

EMOTIONAL LEVEL   96%
INTENSITY   HIGH

Geoffrey read the rest of the printout for brain chemistry function, heart rate, and respiration. Damn. Nick was going into a blind panic.

The doctor looked at Audra's printout and then the printout from the computer in the center:

KEVIN IS LOOKING AT HIS GUN... BLANK EXPRESSION... HE'S STARING AT GERALD'S BODY... FOR HOW LONG?...

FOREVER...

KEVIN'S CLOSING HIS EYES... GUN INSIDE MOUTH... HE FIRED GUN... BLOOD... BODY... SOMEONE... HELP...

END OF MEMORY

"Grab him, Audra!"

"Doing it now."

Click. Click-click, click-click-click. Click. Click.

"I think we almost hot him back," Audra said.

Geoffrey looked at the printout from the computer in front of him. While he waited for Nick's brain function to print, the monitors flashed back on. Audra thought Nick must have moved his head.

"Audio is now a little worse," Audra commented to herself and to her computer.

Geoffrey pressed his recorder to his mouth and began quietly talking into it.

After a few seconds, Audra said, "He's fully out of the memory." She looked at the doctor, but his full attention was on his computer's printout.

Click. Click-click. Click. Click. Click.

* * *

Nick stood by an old rusty stairwell inside the abandon building. From the few remaining crates, Nick surmised that it was a warehouse.

A shadow ran passed overhead of him. Nick looked up and over his left shoulder before he ran up the old stairs. His expensive gym shoes made a padded thud as he ascended. Nick saw the shadow pass along the cinderblock wall to his right and one level above him. Seeing the shadow made Nick clambered up the stairwell that much faster. He gripped the rusty railing with his left hand and held his gun in his right hand.

The printouts read

Do I know how to do this?

Audra continued typing.

Click-click-click-click. Click.

Yeah. Sure. I'm a cop. I'm very good when it comes to shooting.

Geoffrey finished speaking into his recorder. He clicked it off.

"OK, Audra. Bring him up. We'll try next time. May we appease the gods and demigods when they review the all the results. Compared to yesterday's test, today's test was a wash. Make a note in your record for SRT Program 3. We're going to try to manipulate his memories," Dr. Allen said.

The word 'crap' was trying to come out of her mouth, but she managed to stop it. She was a professional and she knew Nick was too. "Bringing him up now." To hell with professionalism. "I'm glad you finally said for me to stop. I was beginning to worry." Then she thought to herself, "Please let Program 3 be OK."

Click-click-click. Click. Click-click, click, click, click. Click-click-click-click.

* * *

Nick was a professional and as part of his requirements to be on the SRT Team, he would make a special note in his report. In

1,000 words or fewer, he would write that from his observations there was a direct correlation between the SRT and his nightmares. Or some other clumsily written paragraph. He wasn't really thinking so well. A few more tests and he would have the proof he needed: SRT usage of more than 4 minutes causes nightmares to the patient when he/she tries to reestablish normal sleeping patterns.

CHAPTER 7

The dreams came frequently to interrupt Nick's nights. They revolved around the four men: James Kurtz and Harold Graham and then Gerald Martin and Kevin Smith. Every time he dreamed about the four men, it was as if Nick were being reminded of past events. He didn't understand why. But, the most horrifying thing was that there was no end to each dream. The murders. Nick would try to scream himself awake. He almost wished that he would see the end of each dream.

Nick started to lose a lot of sleep. After each nightmare, he tried reading until he felt tired. Soon, that didn't work. He tried writing his game after each episode of terror. No, that also didn't work. He finally turned to his work at the SRT lab. That helped him to not fall readily asleep. Eventually, Nick preferred to avoid sleep all together. Getting an average of 5 hours of sleep was OK with him. He was glad that Pete wasn't around much anymore. When he was around, Pete seemed to be a very sound sleeper.

During the winter break, Nick went home. His family was worried about him. He passed of the dark circles around his eyes and pinched face as stress from the SRT project.

For once, Nick was glad that Mid-City's Post-Christmas party was going to be held at the Claye's home. If Nick wasn't so exhausted, he would have noticed the strain on the relationships between the Claye family members during the party.

Nick returned to school on the 3rd of January. That evening, he was back in the lab.

As the winter semester drew on, the SRT project was being refined. The monitors showed the euphemism for memory as 'Residual Matter' and five separate and distinct tests were run. The research team produced results. The gods and demigods were appeased: continued funding for the project was assured.

Just as the SRT was moving along, Nick became more absorbed in his dreams and the SRT project, he started to spend his nights at the lab. This immersion had twisted Nick's version of reality.

To Nick, the dreams became real and tangible. James and Harold, and Gerald and Kevin were real. At first, and for some lucky reason, Nick could hide the beginnings of his psychosis as simply lack of sleep.

During one session, Nick casually referred to the white cylinder shaped SRT machine as the 'Dream Machine'. The name stuck.

It was spring. College students had became entrenched in their social lives. Nick's friends and fellow colleagues assumed he was just overly involved in the project to even have a college social life. Besides, it was time for the party of all parties: SPRING BREAK. But Nick didn't even go home. He only allowed himself brief phone calls with his sister. He used the excuse that he was very busy. Cecily was persistent.

Fate was a strange thing.

* * *

There was going to be a birthday celebration: a little girl's 7th birthday. Mama, Papa, and her two older sisters were around the dining room table. It was early spring. The gas lamps in the room hissed very soothing quiet light on the family.

Mama had baked a special cake. Papa had given her sisters money to pick out the dolly clothes, iron and ironing board for the little girl from Sears and Roebuck's catalogue. The cake and the gifts were a surprise for after dinner.

Papa finished the last bit of food on his plate and sat back. He patted his stomach and told his family that he was glad there was no dessert tonight. He couldn't manage to eat another morsel. The little girl looked very disappointed and her two sisters giggled.

Mama smiled her gentle smile and said, "Well, I better clean the table and dishes. Anna, since it's your birthday, you don't have to help." Mama got up from the table. "Happy birthday, my darling."

Anna was even more disappointed.

"Can I put the ice card in the window, Mama?" said the oldest daughter.

"Yes, why don't you do that. The same amount as last week."

The two older daughters giggled and whispered as they went into the kitchen carrying plates and silverware while Anna looked glumly at her lap. She wanted to be excused from the table and go to her room that she shared with her sisters.

Papa took out his pocket watch and then looked at the black crescents of his finger nails. "Anna, remember to marry a man who likes to do work with his hands. That's the key to happiness. Not someone who does work sitting at a desk in an office. Do you understand?"

"Yes, Papa. But, today's my birthday," Anna said meekly and pensively.

Just then, Mama came out of the kitchen with the cake. Her older sisters were behind their mother carrying her birthday presents.

"Happy birthday, to you!" Anna's family sang. Everyone really made this a special day for her. This was the best birthday, ever.

The family and the dining room dimmed into a blackness. Only Papa was there. But, he was wearing dirty overalls and working on a wheel.

"Mr. Kurtz? What happened to your family?" Nick asked. James Kurtz ignored him; he kept on working on the wheel.

Harold Graham was dressed in a dark brown suit and bowler. Nick could see that he had his right hand hidden. Nick turned to warn James Kurtz what Harold Graham was about to do. But James was gone.

Gerald Martin was sitting behind a desk doing paperwork. Nick was confused; but he wasn't really surprised. For some reason, it made sense to him. He turned away from Gerald and saw Kevin Smith pull a gun out of the jacket of his gray suit.

"You ruined me and this business. When we started, Dynamic Engine was the best. I could've done better without you," said Kevin.

"If I yell for them to stop, would they hear me?" Nick thought.

"Kevin. Please," begged Gerald.

Kevin smiled as he said, "Pleading won't help, Ger." Kevin fired the gun at his partner's chest. The impact made Gerald fall backwards from his chair and onto the floor as Nick had seen several times before in his nightmares.

Then just as before, Nick saw Kevin shooting his partner three more times. Kevin stopped and looked at the gun with a blank expression. Just as before. He opened his mouth as he placed the barrel inside. Just as before. Kevin slowly pulled the trigger then...

Nick was standing in Stan and his father's shop, Mid-City Manufacturer's, Inc.

Stan was in Kevin's gray suit and holding a gun over his father who was sitting at Gerald's desk. Was this supposed to be Stan and Kevin's shop? Stan fired the gun at his partner's chest. The impact made Nick's father fall backwards from his chair and onto the floor.

Nick tried to scream and run to Stan in a tackle-like defense. He couldn't move. He couldn't scream; nothing came from his throat.

Stan/Kevin stopped and looked at the gun with a blank expression. He slowly turned his head and looked at Nick. For the first time in all those dreams, Nick's presence was acknowledged.

"Hey, Nick," Stan/Kevin said with a twisted smile. "You want to see the end? I bet you do. Watch this."

Nick stood there, petrified. He tried to scream himself awake but he couldn't. He couldn't even close his eyes. The same thought roared through his mind: "I'm going to see the end. I'm going to see the end. I'm going to see the end..."

Now it was just Stan with the gun standing before Nick. Stan opened his mouth that was still twisted in a grin. He placed the barrel of the gun in his mouth. Stan slowly pulled the trigger.

"Aw u wathnhk, Nuk," Stan said. There was now an insane gleam in his eyes and a mad expression of tormented delight on his face.

Nick understood clearly that Stan was asking him if he were watching.

Stan took the gun out of his mouth. "Or do you think this gun would look better in your mouth, Nick? Would ya' want to really see the end, huh, Nick. Would ya'?" Now Stan's mouth was an insane, twisted snarl.

"NOOOOOOO!!!!!!!" Nick screamed as he was being shaken awake by his sister.

"Hey," said Cecily as she shook her brother. "Hey, wake up. Wake up!"

"Wha'?" Nick said in that age-old reply. His sister went over to Pete's bed that she was using for the night and sat down. There was some light from the street light outside. The yellowish cast showed that she looked worried about her brother.

"I don't care what lies you're telling Mom and Dad. You can't hide anything from me."

Nick swung his legs out from under the blanket. "Look. You begged me to visit. I don't mind you visiting. I like when you come up and we have fun. But, don't overreact to a bad dream I had."

"A bad dream? No, I don't think it was just a bad dream. I talked to Pete today... Yesterday... He said you woke him up twice in the past three weeks."

"He stays with his girlfriend."

"When he's not with her, he's here. When he's here, you wake him up from your screaming."

"It was only a dream. I'm all right." He had thought his roommate was a sound sleeper. Apparently not.

"You're not all right."

"Yes. *I am*," Nick was annoyed by his sister's prodding. He dismissed her concern by pulling the blanket back on himself and rolling away from her to face the wall. "I'm fine."

"Tomorrow... Today you're going to see a counselor."

"No, I'm not. Let me get back to sleep."

Cecily came over to him and shook his shoulder. "Then I'm telling Mom and Dad."

"No." Nick said as he rolled onto his back to look up into his sister's tired and worried face. Her brow was worry wrinkled. Their mother had that same look when she was worried. "It's just the project I'm working on. It's very intense. There's a lot to do."

"So it *is* the project. I thought…" She didn't know what to think. Her brother said it was only a computer program that he was helping to write.

"Nick had cut her off, "If word gets around, then there goes the funding and my work. And any chances at a half-way decent high paying job."

"So again. The project. Everything comes back to it. I should've guessed a lot sooner. What good would it do you if you end up in the hospital from exhaustion?"

"Crap," he thought, "Some of me *had* to rub off on to her now of all times." Then out loud he said, "It's not going to happen. I'm fine." He rolled over again to face the wall. Cecily grabbed his shoulder and tried to pull him on to his back. He waved his arm in a "leave-me-alone" motion.

"How about one of my friends I met from work last summer? He's in art school now."

"News flash. Your friend is from an art school. Not a medical- or psychiatric school. *Therefore*, he's one of the 'wanna be beautiful people'."

Cecily decided to ignore her brother's biting remark, even though she usually wouldn't allow anyone—even Nick—to demean her future chosen profession. "He's into dream interpretations and all that stuff."

"Great," Nick mumbled. "A witch doctor in the make."

"Then I'm going to let Mom and Dad know exactly how things're going with you."

Did he have a choice? Really?

Before he fell back to sleep, he thought about the time when they were younger. They really hated each other and were constantly at each other. She always accused their parents of favoring Nick because he was so smart and was in a private school for kids like himself. He always accused their parents of favoring Cecily. She got away with a lot of things that he knew he would *never* be able to get away with.

One summer when he was going to be sixteen and his sister was 13 years old, they went to two different camps. Cecily went to a general camp and he went to a camp for the gifted. Two weeks into the summer, she was sent home. She couldn't stand the constant headache that she continually complained of having to the camp-counselors and nurse. Like a typical older brother, when Nick learned of Cecily's *headache*, he assumed that it was just another ploy for their parents' attention.

He quickly changed his mind when he was told a day or so later by his father that Cecily was put in the hospital for spinal meningitis. He asked to come home. For the first time, he realized that he loved his sister. He was afraid that he was going to lose her during that one summer.

CHAPTER 8

A portable fan droned in front of a window and between the two beds of the small dorm room. Nick and Cecily sat on one of the beds. It was the second day of a very warm spell in spring. Unframed art work covered one half of the wall above them. Opposite of Nick and Cecily, unframed photographs covered the other wall. Someone, Nick couldn't decide if it was Cecily's friend or her friend's roommate, had managed to get an old pair of boots, three used text books and a pencil to stay on the ceiling. The objects looked like they were casually left there by their owner. A ceiling lamp was placed in the middle of the floor.

Cecily saw her brother stare at the ceiling. "Self expression," she commented.

"And you think I'm having problems?"

"Hey!" said a young man who just entered the small dorm room with an old backpack. He was momentarily surprised at the two in his room. But, his face brightened when he saw his friend,

Cecily. "I got the stuff. Now we can start," He closed the door and pulled out a six-pack of the cheapest beer he could buy from the bag. He was wearing torn, paint-stained jeans, an old Harley-Davidson T-shirt, a pair of sun glasses, and a red bandanna around his head. In spite of his appearance, he was clean shaven.

"Bing let us in. I thought it'd be cool with you," said Cecily.

"Yeah. It's cool. I'm John. Want one?" He asked holding up the six-pack by the plastic rings.

"No, thanks." Nick replied.

"Yeah," Cecily said. "No tossing."

John smiled at her. It was obvious to Nick that a lot of tossed beers had fizzed and splattered his sister before. Nick looked at his sister. Now he had something over her: she wasn't old enough to be legally drinking.

John tapped the top of his can before he opened it. "OK. Tell me everything. Ces told me some. But I need more."

"Look. I'm doing this to shut Cecily up."

"Thanks." His sister answered with sarcasm.

"So start." John took off his glasses and placed them on a shelf. He sat down on his bed and started drinking from his can.

He didn't want to humor his sister anymore. Nick got up and started to walk for the door.

"Do it and I'm making that call." Cecily said to her brother's back.

"Don't you have a can of beer in your hands?"

"Hey, hey. Play nice. Come on, Nick, have a seat. Relax. You can trust me."

Did he have a choice? Nick stopped and turned around to face his sister and her friend. He sat down again next to his sister before he began telling them from the time of the first nightmare from the first SRT test to the present nightmare. He left out any vital information that would seem as if he were divulging in privileged information about the program.

There were now three cans of empty beer and one empty bottle of soda by John's bed when Nick was done retelling his dreams. Somewhere in the middle of retelling the nightmares, Nick asked for a can of beer. Just having to think about them was giving him the 'heeby-jeebs.'

The only sound in the room when Nick was done telling John his dreams was the 'ssssurrrr' of the droning fan. Then John let out a loud cheap beer belch.

"You pig!" Cecily looked at her friend in disgust.

"I could've farted!" John let out a muted burp and patted his chest twice with the inside of his fist. "'Cuse, me." He gave Cecily an insincere toothy smile and made his blue eyes look sweetly innocent. He liked to tease her.

"Oh, please," Nick mumbled. He lowered his head and pinched the bridge of his nose with his thumb and index finger. Why did he allow himself to be here in the first place?

"I was right."

Nick looked up and saw that Cecily's friend was very serious. When Nick was retelling his dreams, John seemed to be more interested in empting a beer can. Nick now knew there was more to John than he suspected. John was an intense person in spite of his appearance.

John continued, "This happened before."

"I really don't believe all that kind of crap." Nick said as he looked into John's blue eyes and saw that Cecily's friend was *very* serious.

"Look. Your father got screwed over by his partner in two different past lives. I guess he didn't do good. In business. And each time, one or the other tried to even the score. I can bet anything that it's going to happen again. You're here now because you didn't do it before and you want to break the cycle." John said. Nick looked at Cecily's friend as if he were really crazy. "I'm bein' honest here."

"Our father is a *damn* good business man!" Cecily looked annoyed by her friend's comment.

"I didn' say he wasn'. I just said that in his past lives he made a few mistakes."

Nick didn't like the flippant remark that John made. Cecily's friend or not. And, she just sat there calmly. Screw it! He should just walk out now. But something made him want to stay.

"Then how do we stop it from happening this time?" Cecily asked John.

"You're kidding me, right?" Nick looked at his sister as if she were just as crazy as her friend.

"Don't know. Do you, Nick?"

"No." Nick tried to regain some of his composure.

"Yes, you do. Or rather you will know when the time comes. You just haven' re-experienced that part yet." John said.

"Huh."

CHAPTER 9

"NO!!!" Yelled Nick, as Gerald Martin fell backwards from his chair and onto the floor. There was blood everywhere. Nick thought he could smell the blood and the smoke from Kevin Smith's gun.

Nick saw Kevin shooting his partner three more times. Kevin looked at the gun with a blank expression. He closed his eyes as he placed the gun to his opened mouth and then he fired...

"NOOOOOO!!!" Nick sat straight up in his bed screaming. he quickly looked around his dark room. The slow shadows from a passing car's lights played on his walls and Nick concentrated on them to calm his nerves. When his breathing returned to normal, he realized he was drenched in sweat.

His roommate said, "Umphmm," and then rolled over to face the wall on his side of the room. Nick could see by the regular raise and fall of Pete's upper body that he was fast asleep again.

The only time Nick and Pete actually did see each other was in passing when going to class or returning from class.

Nick laid back down and thought about the final SRT he was going to do tomorrow—or rather later on that day.

"Yes, you do. Or rather you will know when the time comes. You just haven' re-experienced that part yet," Nick heard John say to him in an absurdly decorated dorm room from that afternoon. Or was it several days ago?

CHAPTER 10

"GET HIM AWAY!!! GET HIM AWAY!!! STOP!!! STOP!!!"
The words could be seen on the monitors as well as heard from
the SRT machine (Dream Machine). Nicholas Colemore, Jr. was
inside of the machine in the smaller white room screaming and
clawing the leads off of his head and body. He finally saw the end.

"Damn!" Yelled Dr. Allen as he pressed a button by his
monitor and leaned into the speaker. "Two aides! Now! Bring a
gurney!" Dr. Allen looked over to Audra. She was frantically
keying in data on her keyboard. "Is he responding?"

"No," answered Audra. She continued to type at a maddening
pace.

The monitors showed

Help me!!! He's coming after me!!!

over and over

Help me!!! He's coming after me!!!

The data that spat out on the printers showed that the doctor's and technician's attempts at erasing the past few SRT induced memories were a futile and dismal failure.

The screaming grew worse. Audra, without stopping from entering data, looked through the window at the Dream Machine. Geoffrey followed Audra's stare. Both, the doctor and the technician looked gaped-mouthed as the Machine seemed to rock and jig as if it were something from an animated cartoon.

Damn it! He couldn't wait for the aides. Dr. Allen filled an injection gun with a tranquillizer and pushed open the door to the little white room. Dr. Allen threw open the top of the Dream Machine and began to wrestle with Nick. Leads and arms seemed to fly everywhere.

Two aides came in to hold down the screaming volunteer. Dr. Allen didn't waste the opportunity to sedate Nick.

"Take him to the infirmary put him in an exam room and restrain him when you're there."

"Infirmary?" One aide questioned. Two new isolation rooms were just completed by private funding.

"The infirmary before he wakes up." Repeated the doctor.

The two aides quickly glanced at each other as they lifted Nick onto the gurney and covered him with a blanket. Nick was babbling and twitching in a drug sedated sleep as he was being wheeled out of the lab.

With regret, Dr. Allen felt that he had failed miserably. He couldn't help restore the mind of one of the best college students the university ever had. He had to finally admit to himself that Nick needed help. Most importantly, he had to have Willis Pearson, his superior, admit that Nick needed help. Nicholas Colemore, Jr. had finally lost his sanity and his grasp of reality while taking the final Synaptic Reflex Control Test. It was six months ago that Geoffrey thought that Nick was assisting the scientific community and him through this wonderful breakthrough. Dr. Geoffrey Allen wanted so badly for the SRTs to be successful. He truly believed that SRTs could be used in the future as a cure for psychiatric disorders from mild neurosis to the criminally insane. Now he was faced with the fact that he failed himself: he had compromised his integrity. Worse of all, he was faced with a worse failure than his own. He had turned one of the best minds he had ever known into glop. The doctor went back into the control room.

"Give me everything. The CDs. Printouts. Results. Everything," said Dr. Allen.

"I'm just finishing," replied Audra without stopping to look at the doctor. She wouldn't allow herself to cry now.

"He'll get the best of care. He'll get better." Geoffrey made the comment more for his own behalf than for Audra's.

"Here," said Audra as she handed the doctor several CDs. "Will you let me know when I can visit him?"

"Thanks. I will." Dr. Allen went down to his office. He sat in front of his computer to review the last twenty minutes of Nick's test and performance during what was supposed to be a full run of a Synaptic Reflex Control Test. This SRT, if everything was going to go the way it should have gone would be the final product. No dress rehearsal. Geoffrey made notes to update the volunteer's chart before he called the director of the medical school and his superior, Dr. Willis Pearson to discuss Nick's admission to one of the best psychiatric hospitals in the country at the expense of I-N, Inc. Maybe Nick could at least gather what was left of his brains and work a simple menial job or maybe function in a workshop for the mentally disadvantaged. Crap.

Geoffrey wanted the director to see first hand how Nick had deteriorated from a promising future bio-physicist to a young man who babbled insensately about guns, blood, and death while walking around the campus for the past three days in a stiff gate and sunken eyes.

There was a time when a little boy had kept digging a deep hole by the huge tree in the family's backyard. That little boy thought he did...

"What the hell do you think you're doing?! I just came from the infirmary. Why is Nick there!? What happened to him?! He looks like he had a fight with a pack of wild dogs!" Dr. Pearson yelled as he gruffly entered the office and slammed the door.

"I felt that I should closely monitor him." Geoffrey hoped that his reply was calm and steady. He didn't feel that way. "I have him heavily sedated. He was trying to claw the leads off of himself during this past SRT session. I'll have him moved to the hospital in an hour."

"Bullcrap! I see you're still trying to have him be dismissed from the testing. We can't. I told you before his father is a sponsor to the school. One of his uncles' a senator of this state. Either of those two finds out about the mess you've made this project, we'll both have our asses nailed to a wall and this place will be closed down. God only knows what I-N will do to us now!" The director was in a red-faced rage. His fists were clenched.

Geoffrey thought that if his superior got any angrier, he would end up putting his 60 year-old heart in a sling. As it was, Geoffrey tried to clean the mess up and now it was too late. It was his superior's urging that Geoffrey select Nick and his insistence that he keep Nick on the project. Dr. Allen knew that Dr. Pearson was going to make him take full responsibility for this miserable failure. He quickly thought of a way to protect and help Nick. "Pull up a chair. I want you to see today's test results. The raw data will help us when you and I talk to I-N tomorrow."

The director humored him. Good, at least the man is curious enough. Or maybe it was a case of covering one's ass.

"I was told by I-N that recording and then taking care of a memory would be easy. We made that breakthrough a year ago. You were *supposed* to have done *that!* After we saw all out limits! That's why we have you here." The director was still angry. Here comes that bus and Geoffrey was being pushed right under it. "You're damn lucky I've time for this crap," replied Dr. Pearson as he pulled up a chair next to Dr. Allen and sat down.

Dr. Allen slipped in the first CD that read: 'Nicholas Colemore, Jr.'s SRT #1' into the computer's disk drive and typed the necessary commands. He glanced at his notes at the numbers marking the place that had the particular recording that he wanted to show the director.

"Before we get to today's test, we need to review the pattern again. Colemore's first SRT was OK. Normal amount of residual matter with the normal percent of emotional level. Nothing out of the ordinary in the first half of the program." Dr. Allen pointed to the lower portion of the computer monitor to emphasize his point. Then resumed typing.

The monitor went from

BLACK

then blinked to

GRAY
GRAY
WHITE

as Dr. Allen found the particular recorded program and memory that he needed.

"I'm going to skip around a lot. Please excuse some of the hazy visual and audio. We had technical difficulties here," Dr. Allen said as he continued to key in the necessary commands. The segment he wanted was 42-950. The director just gave him a disgusted look.

The monitor showed

SYNAPTIC REFLEX TEST
PROTOTYPE
PROGRAM ONE

Police Simulation Program
in the center of the screen. In the right lower corner the numbers

42-950

blinked.

"Almost there." Dr. Allen continued typing.

The monitor showed

BLACK

42-980

then showed

GRAY
GRAY

Dr. Pearson settled back in his chair to view Nick's recordings including recordings of some of Nick's inner thoughts which had initially came over the monitors during the SRTs were also recorded. Everything was in Nick's point of view. Being able to review the subject's inner thoughts was a problem that will need to be rectified later.

Nick carefully walked through the shadow-casted halls. He gripped his gun to reassure himself. Inside the machine, Nick's left hand seemed to grip an imaginary gun. He looked at the shadow play against the walls. He quickly aimed to shoot, then stopped. He thought he saw someone. It was only the moonlight through the trees outside of the opposite window. The light and shadows fell against a picture of a teen-aged girl on the wall. The effect momentarily gave the picture animation and from the corner of his eye, it seemed that another person was with him in the hall.

Teen-aged girl. My sister. We used to fight when we were kids. Light.

MEMORY

Nick and his sister were sitting on the concrete and granite steps of the fine arts building where Cecily hoped to attend school. It was a sunny day with a slight breeze that trailed down the busy city street. Students carrying huge book bags or art portfolios scrambled in and out of the huge double doors of the building.

"I sometimes feel Dad is still upset with me," said Nick.

A college student dropped his book bag at the bottom of the step and swung his guitar case around from his back, took it off and opened it to begin playing. A few strums of tuning joined Nick and Cecily's conversation. The college student began to play.

"To be honest, he would rather see you taking over the shop. But, he said it's OK doing what you're doing," answered Cecily.

"Truck and car engine parts never enthused me."

"I know."

The two doctors observed Nick taking in the immediate surroundings.

"The kid on guitar is good, commented Dr. Pearson. "I happen to like jazz."

Nick and his sister stopped talking for a while. Instead they watched students and visitors pass by during the late spring day. A young woman started to play the saxophone.

"The girl's good too." Said Dr. Allen.

"Why did you choose to go into physics?" his sister asked.

The doctors listened to the conversation as an ambulance screeched in a panicked cry round the corner. In front of him, a taxi honked before speeding away from the curb. All the extraneous sights and sounds were registered in Nick's mind and duly noted in a part of his brain for him to remember or not to remember. However, Nick did take notice of a man in an old army coat who took out his guitar and started to play a few strings with the first two musicians.

Nick shrugged his shoulders, then leaned back against the step above him. "Physics with bio-engineering. Because I'm good at it. It's that the usual reason? I don't really want to take over Dad's business. Not with Stan around and I really don't like Stan's sons enough to want to be their partners. But then again, I could ask you why you're going to art school and not taking over the business too."

A sound of another helicopter flew overhead.

"Because I'm good at art. I'm an artist." Cecily stood up. "Where else can I get away with dressing the way I want to? I made it myself." She spun around and then sat back down.

Nick smiled. "Yep. You did. You blend in with the crowd. In fact all you artsy-fartsy students look like Picasso threw up on you."

The two doctors were amused by the exchange even when Nick's sister gave him the middle finger and her rebuttal.

Dr. Allen typed in the commands to end this particular segment.

The monitor blinked

BLACK
BLACK

then

GRAY
WHITE

as Dr. Allen keyed in the next recording for viewing.

"This is SRT #2. The first real deviation from the program. You'll see when I run it that the data from the scans don't match. It's as if the memory is not really his own, but superimposed.

"What are you saying?" asked the Director.

"Look." Answered Dr. Allen.

WHITE

then it showed

47-011

the monitor blinked

BLACK
BLACK
GRAY

The recorded test played for the two men. Dr. Allen put his index finger on the lower part of the computer showing the Nick's functions. "Now here's where Nick starts to deviate in the Program. Notice the spiking from the brain activity and the SRT output. Neither one will coincide at the same time. That's where the memory seemed to be superimposed."

BLACK
GRAY
GRAY
WHITE

The Director tried to process everything he just saw. "Unbelievable. Remarkable."

"The next one is much worse and more 'remarkable.'"

Geoffrey thought that his choice of using his superior's comment of 'remarkable' was appalling to him. How can anything that had caused the bright young man's mind to deteriorate to be seen as only as 'remarkable'. "I need to change CDs." (Coins and gems found in a hole by a big tree.) Dr. Allen exchanged CDs then typed the commands on the computer's keyboard.

69-003

WHITE

BLACK

BLACK

GRAY

GRAY

The recorded program showed Nick watching the interchange between Gerald Martin and Kevin Smith. There was a spike of activity in the lower part of the computer.

Dr. Pearson was shocked to see the internal thought from Nick flash on the screen: *They don't see or hear me. It's just like with James Kurtz and Harold Graham.*

Dr. Pearson looked at Dr. Allen, "Why does Nick remember from one test to another. I thought you erased each program from him."

"We thought we did. We were successful with the other volunteers. But not with Nick. It may be due to his higher than average intelligence." Dr. Allen exchanged the current CD for another CD.

The monitor soon showed

WHITE
BLACK
BLACK

then

GRAY
BLACK
BLACK
WHITE

176-555

The two doctors watched a segment of the recorded program. When it was over, Dr. Allen exchanged the CD to play the final test that resulted in Nick's current state.

The monitor soon showed

WHITE
BLACK
BLACK
GRAY

then

801-202

"Wait a minute! We just saw this. Do you have the right CD in?" Asked Dr. Pearson.

"It's the right one. Really strange. Isn't it? Every step, every nuance is repeated." For emphasis, Dr. Allen showed Dr. Pearson the printouts.

A flicker came on the small section of the monitor as the two men looked at two lines of a printout. The flicker only lasted a few seconds. If both men were watching the monitor at that particular moment, they would have seen Stan's face. It was the same flicker that Dr. Allen and Audra Kramer missed during the initial run of the test because they were too pre-occupied with the erratic output and were busy trying to stabilize Nick to look.

flicker

Gerald was begging for his life. Kevin fired the gun at his partner's chest.

"NO!!!" Nick saw the body fall. He saw blood splatter around on the desk and the chair

that

The chair swiveled to face the door. I think I see Gerald's arm from behind the desk. It has blood on it.

Kevin looked at the gun with a blank expression. He closed his eyes and placed the gun to his open mouth. Kevin was about to shoot himself. He stopped and opened his eyes.

It's not goin' to happen this time.

Kevin took the gun away from his mouth, turned to Nick

and aimed the gun at him. Kevin started to walk towards Nick with a twisted smile. The smile almost seemed to curl into a snarl.

Dr. Pearson sat forward in his chair as he saw the top half of the monitor look like the recording was sped up by 80% while the bottom half was going just as wild with data.

"It would look better in 'your' mouth."

HE SEES ME! NO!!!

The last audio recording of Nicholas Colemore, Jr., promising physicist and bio-engineer: "GET HIM AWAY!!! GET HIM AWAY!!! STOP!!! STOP!!!"

Dr. Pearson just stared at the blank monitor in disbelief before sitting back and rested his elbows on the arms of his chair. He hands were together with the sides of his index fingers lightly touching his mouth. He looked like he was praying. After a few moments, he dropped his hands to his lap and looked at Dr. Allen. "Hospitalization." He wanted to be physically ill.

"Hospitalization and intensive psychiatric treatments. *Traditional, non-evasive* psychiatric treatments. I already have a doctor waiting at the hospital for Nick."

"I'll be the one to tell his father what happened to his son. We'll be lucky if his family doesn't have 'our guts for lunch'. I'm sure after I-N is done with us, we'll be glad to be hand fed to the media circus." He would need to retire and Dr. Allen can examine a career in flipping burgers.

* * *

In a room somewhere in Nick's pharmacologically induced slurred thoughts he made the connection that he had to leave. He couldn't. He couldn't move his arms or legs. But, he really felt too good to leave anyway. Maybe he would sleep awhile. Sleep would be good.

CHAPTER 11

Nick and his doctor—referred by everyone as Neil—were in a session. Things were a little different this time. Nick was looking forward to going home. He now knew for a fact that Kevin won't be there. This was a lot of improvement from five months ago. It was almost a year ago. Wait. Has it been a year? When he first came to the hospital, he *knew* that Harold was one of the floor's aides.

"Do your dreams scare you?"

"No. They're just dreams." Nick wanted to emphasize the comment with a shrug. He hoped that his therapist believed that to Nick dreams were not real: especially dreams of the four men.

"Do you really believe that? Now?" Neil felt his patient did, but it was no harm to really be sure.

Nick shrugged. "They're just dreams."

"Do you think you're ready to go home?"

"I would like to try. Yeah. I'm ready."

"Good. I'll write up the discharge first thing tomorrow. I know that your family is looking forward to seeing you. I expect you to see me on an out-patient basis." As Neil got up, he extended his right hand. "I wish you all the luck."

"Thanks." Nick shook Neil's hand.

CHAPTER 12

Nick was standing by one of the deburring machines in the shop of Mid-City Manufacturers. Across half of the floor he could see his father doing paperwork at the desk by the door to the offices. Nicholas Colmore, Sr. stopped writing and looked to his left at Nick.

"Nicky, you've got to help us." Only his father called him 'Nicky'.

"How, Dad?" Nick said. But his father went back to his work. Nick had a feeling that his father no longer saw him.

Stan came through the door. When he stood in front of the desk he pulled out a gun from his gray suit.

"You've ruined this business. You brought Mid-City down with you. You son-uf-a-bitch." Stan fired the gun at his partner's chest. The impact made his father fall backwards from his chair and onto the floor.

Nick tried to scream and run to Stan in a tackle-like defense of his father. He couldn't move, nothing came from his mouth. All Nick could do is watch Stan shoot his father three more times. Then just like Harold and Kevin, Stan stopped and looked at the gun with a blank expression before he opened his mouth as he placed the barrel inside. Stan slowly pulled the trigger and then stopped. He took the gun away from his mouth and looked at Nick.

"Do you think this gun would look better in your mouth?" Stan said with an insane, twisted smile. He started walking towards Nick. Nick tried to move backwards. Maybe he could run for the loading dock and escape that way. But Nick couldn't move his feet. He couldn't scream.

"NOOOOOOO!!!!!!!" Nick tried to scream himself away. It was the only thing that escaped from his throat.

"Not this time, you bastard. I'm going to make sure I get you this time." Stan said with his insane and twisted smile. Yet, he spoke very calmly, evenly.

"No, Stan, not this time either," said a shadow to Nick's right. The shadow moved towards Nick and Stan to reveal that is was James Kurtz. Both, Stan and Nick could only look gap-mouthed at James who was wearing a very neat suit of his period. "Don't bother trying to turn the gun on me either." Said James who now was Gerald. "Nicky, you've got to help us. Today, this morning at 6:30. Please help us," said Gerald who now was his father.

* * *

Nick came to Mid-City at 5:43, according to his car's clock. Part of the agreement he had with his doctor was that he wasn't supposed to be behind the wheel of a car. But, then again, he wasn't supposed to allow his father get murdered by his partner either. Nick parked his car two-and-a-half blocks away in the industrial park and walked to the loading dock of Mid-City. He was dressed like any other truck driver and he made sure the bill of his baseball cap was low enough to hide his face from the security camera. Once he got into the building, he thought he would hide and wait by one of the deburring machines.

CHAPTER 13

Nick sat in a huddled position making sure that the cold early morning sun wouldn't cast his shadow against the dirty cement floor. He waited. The cold seemed to try to work its way through his sneakers and up his legs. The chill was also working its way through the two heavy jersey jackets he wore. The material of his regular winter coat made of a synthetic scraping noise. Nick hoped that the winter bitterness wouldn't make his legs cramp before he had to…

Nick heard the shop door screech open. Heavy work boots clumped on the floor and stopped. One of the smaller machines started with a thrum. Nick then heard the door screech again. He was alone once more.

He looked at his watch. 6:12. The door screeched again. By the sound of the treading feet and the early hour, it was either his father or Stan. Nick stood up only enough to get a glimpse of the person by not enough to be detected. He blew in his cupped hands to warm them. It was his father who was now at a desk by Final Inspection. He was organizing a few folders. Nick crouched down again and looked at his watch.

6:27.

The door screeched open again.

"Stan. Good morning." Nick heard his father in a congenial and even tone. "I'll be ready in a minute. If the guys get here before 7:00, maybe you can get them coffee. I started a pot up front. Sue will be bringing donuts and bagels. Dave just left."

Nick stood up again to see what was happening. As before, he made sure neither man would see him. He rubbed and massaged his legs as quietly as he could, hoping that would bring back some of the circulation to them. Still in a semi-crouching position, he started to weave his way closer to the desk. He hoped that the machines he chose to conceal himself behind would be good choices. He was finally directly behind the two men. Nick had guessed that he was almost 3 feet away.

He almost lost his balance when he tried to avoid a pile of rejected parts. His right arm shot out and grabbed the leg of a table to regain his equilibrium. No noise made. At least Stan still had his back to him. He looked at his right arm and without thinking at the watch that peaked out of the sleeves of two jersey jackets.

6:28.

Now Nick looked again at the two men. Stan had a gun aimed at his father.

"Wha'?" Nick heard his father say.

"You f-king, son-ufa-bitch. I could've done better without you."

All of Nick's muscles tensed. Now he knew exactly what he was supposed to do.

"NOOO!!!" Yelled Nick as he sprung up and ran to tackle his father's partner.

Stan heard someone yell behind him. Without thinking, he spun around and fired a single bullet.

Nick felt hot pain in his chest as he fell backwards from the impact. Everything became blurred for him. His chest hurt. It was hard to breath. He must have had the wind knocked out of him when he fell backwards. Everything became blurred for him. Faces swarmed round him. What time is it?

Someone had slipped something over his face, while another person was trying to do something to his chest. Why?

Then he slept.

"Thank you," said a voice from behind him. Nick turned around and saw a man he had never seen before.

"What?"

"Thank you. You broke the cycle," said the man. He was middle-aged. Yet, his hair was all gray. He looked as if he hadn't shaven in two days. The man was dressed in old, worn jeans and a faded gray polo shirt. His sneakers were worn with holes by the toes.

Nick's only reply was a puzzled look.

"Let's take a walk while I explain. I'm Ed by the way."

The two started to walk down a deserted hospital corridor.

Nick noticed there was no sound. He couldn't even hear their footfalls or the hollow echo of Ed's voice. But he should have been able to hear some kind of sound other than Ed's echoless voice. He wondered about this.

After they turned and entered another deserted corridor, Ed broke the silence. "Do you believe in past lives?"

"No," Nick said flatly. After all, his beliefs were firmly entrenched in the sciences.

"Too bad," Ed replied. They continued to walk a little slower without speaking. Then Ed stopped and turned to Nick. "Harold killed James because their business was going bankrupt. In actuality, times were bad and Harold was really a poor business man to begin with. If those two stayed with it a little longer, things would have worked out."

"But one of my sister's friends said…"

Ed gave a dry chuckle. "That kid has a long way to go before he completely understands. He shouldn't have even said anything like that when he didn't know what he was talking about in the first place. But, he was pretty close. I'll give him that." he shrugged. "'Half an idea is better than none.'

"As I was saying, I left off with… Harold killed James because…bankruptcy… Oh, yeah. Business would get better if those two stuck things out. But Harold couldn't see beyond that. Maybe if psychology were better known than." Ed stopped to think about the absurdity of the situation that Harold had put himself in. He turned to Nick, who looked curious as to why Ed was smiling. "Umphj. Oh, well. Shall we continue?" Ed and Nick started to walk down the corridor again.

A few steps were taken. "If there was a psychologist in town back then Harold would've been diagnosed as being, shall we say, 'paranoid.'"

"I think anyone could've seen that he was crazy. Even back then," Nick commented.

"True. Years later, Harold came back as Kevin and you came back as Gerald. Kevin was to kill Gerald and..."

"Wait a minute. The SRTs."

"I know. A month from now Geoffrey will discover that he had simulated one of the effects of narcoepilepsy..."

"...The dreamer being able to see him-or herself in a dream." Nick finished Ed's sentence. "Are you a doctor?"

Ed smiled and gave Nick a coy 'I don't know' shrug, palms up. Then Nick noticed Ed's hands. They were very clean and free of calluses. His fingernails were well-groomed. Ed's clean and well groomed hands were incongruous with the stubble on his face and his shabby clothes.

"They match everyone up."

"Who're *they?*" Nick saw by Ed's expression that he shouldn't press any further.

"Where was I?..."

"I think you left off where I came back as Gerald. Kevin to kill Gerald," Nick was getting impatient.

"Yeah. Gerald. There's a third party missing, you see. The shop boy who fell asleep the night before in the barn and saw

Harold kill James. Now here's where it gets 'interesting'. At least for me. James came back as another little shop boy to prevent Kevin from killing Gerald."

"But he doesn't succeed," Nick said.

"Nope. So, we're back again where we started."

"Wait a minute. Stan is really Harold? And I'm really James?" Nick asked.

"Almost got it. Stan is Harold. But, your father is James. And you're the shop boy.

"All along Harold was insane enough not to learn from the first life experience. And unfortunately, he took James right along with him. Because James wanted his partner—in more ways than one—to learn and move one."

"But Harold wouldn't," Nick said.

"Harold *couldn't*. Let's sit down in here," Ed said. They approached an empty waiting room. As they sat down on an old and worn blue vinyl couch, Ed continued. "James thought he could break the cycle as the shop boy the second time around. He tried though. Not very successful.

"Then it was going to be the third time around. Something had to be done and done right."

"Why?"

"Can't say right now. You'll find out. But now is not the time to know. Believe me." Ed rested his elbows on his knees and gave his chin a good scratch before he continued. "It was the third time around and the situation had to be corrected. It was, shall we say, that it was no coincidence that you liked physics and bioengineering. It was finally you who broke the cycle." Ed straightened himself before he stood up and walked out of the waiting room. Nick followed him. Both walked down the corridor in silence.

Finally, Nick spoke, "It was planned like that? Me breaking the cycle."

"More or less."

"Now what?"

The two men stopped at a pair of double doors that lead to another corridor.

"Go through these doors," Ed said as he gave himself another quick scratch. "and it's up to you. We all have choices that we are given during our lives. You chose to break the cycle. Now things can move on the way they should have during that one time so long ago.

"You can return to your life and continue. Or. Or, you can not return and continue."

"What happens to Stan?" Nick asked.

"Prison for the criminally insane. The Synaptic Reflex Control Programs you were helping to be developed will be coming into good use."

Nick nodded his head in appreciation. Choices. "I'll miss my friends and family on one hand and on another I won't. If I choose to go back to my life…I wonder how good a physicist I would be?…" Nick trailed off into his thoughts.

Ed shrugged his shoulders. "Up to you," he said.

"What if I go back that way?" Nick asked, thumbing towards the corridor the two men just walked through.

"Not an option."

Nick looked at the doors. He turned to his companion and gave him his hand to shake.

"Thanks again, Nick."

"You're welcome. I'm glad it turned out the way it did."

Nicholas Colemore, Jr. pushed the double doors open and walked through.

His choice.

Rabbitt Whole

She didn't know how she ended up sitting on a hard bench in a police station. She didn't remember her name.

Why am I wearing this white formal gown? She looked at her well pedicured toes strapped by shoes that could feed a family of four for three weeks. Her expensive formal gown probably could feed the same family for three months.

She looked at her left wrist and rubbed it. Why was it bare? She knew that it should have jewelry on it. Her bare wrist gave her a glimpse of a memory…

A man in a tuxedo was fastening the clasp of a beautiful gold bracelet with a charm around her left wrist. Who was the man? Why was he in a tuxedo? She couldn't see his face.

A policeman came over to her. "I'm sorry ma'am for keepin' you so long. Here's your bag." He handed her a small silver and white purse that matched her gown. "We're checkin' the database now for your husband's location."

Husband? I'm married. The man in the tuxedo. But I don't remember what he looks like.

Another policeman came over and ushered the first officer away. She could see them glance at her occasionally as they had a discussion in low tones.

What happened tonight?

The two officers walked away and she felt alone again. She opened her small clutch for her mints. *Mints! I like mints because I gave up smoking last year... How do I know that?*

There would be an ID in her purse. A phone.

A man in a simple suit walked up to her. He offered her his hand to shake. "I'm Detective Mikelson. Why don't we talk privately?" He ushered her into an office. "I don't think the Captain will mind if we borrow his office for a while." He closed the door behind him.

"Would you like some coffee?"

"No, thank you. I would like to go home and wait for my husband."

"Husband? You must be mistaken. According to our check, you're not married. You're not wearing a wedding ring."

"But the two officers..." She looked at her left hand then at the closed door and made a feeble attempt at finishing her sentence. She was still looking at the door when she said, "Why am I here? Am I being charged with anything?" She was almost hoping her questions would be answered by someone on the other side.

"Charged? Why do you say that?"

She looked away from the door to answer the detective. He was not wearing the simple suit—he was wearing a white lab coat and had a stethoscope around his neck. She saw his ID on his chest pocket, *Dr. A. Mikelson.*

"But this is a police station." She said in a feeble voice.

"No. You were in a police station earlier and now you're here in Good Shepard Hospital, North."

She looked around. *This isn't an office. I'm on a hospital exam table in an emergency room.* "What happened?" She was still clutching her little purse.

"There was a car accident...."

She woke up. It took a moment to for her to gain her orientation. She was in a hospital room. The bed next to hers was empty. She could see nurses and aides hurry past her doorway. One of the nurses stopped in to look at her before entering.

"Good!" The nurse gave her a warm smile before entering. "You're awake. You gave us quite a scare the past two nights. The doctor will be in later on to see you. You're friend is waiting outside. He's been by every day."

"How long?" The sound of her whispering-croaking voice startled her.

"Six days. The past two days you were trying very hard to come back to us." The nurse was checking the woman's I.V. and monitors. "Do you want to see your friend?"

"OK." She didn't have any idea who her friend might be. Maybe he would take her home. Her head was beginning to hurt. "I want a mirror." She whisper-croaked again.

"Are you sure?" The nurse seemed to want to protect her.

The woman tried to nod. A new stab of pain shot through the

back of her neck to her forehead.

"Careful. Even with a brace you're going to be sore." The nurse handed her a small mirror from the woman's bedside nightstand.

The reflection horrified her. Her eyes were black and blue. Her swollen lips were cut and bruised on her right side of her face. Her forehead was bandaged.

The nurse left and a medium built man in jeans and a polo shirt came in to the room. He had a vase of wildflowers.

"Emma!" He put the vase on her stand. "The doctor told me last week that you may have amnesia from the accident." He paused. "Do you know who I am?"

Emma. My name is Emma. She thought.

Her visitor looked uncomfortable by her non-reply. "The flowers are your favorite." He looked around for something else to say.

Emma looked quickly at the vase full of multicolored blooms. She could tell that her friend knew she didn't remember by her passive expression.

She finally had to ask, "Who are you?" *Did I insult him? I thought I saw him look hurt just now.*

"I'm Bob Mullen. We've been friends since college."

"Oh." She looked at the foot of the bed. "Will you take me home when I'm ready?" She looked at him again.

"Absolutely! Since you don't have a car any more and …" Bob was trying to find a gentle way of stating it. "You need to regain your strength and health. I'll help you any way you want.

I'll run over to your place and pick up some clean clothes and anything else you want when you're ready to leave here."

"Thanks." She tried a feeble smile through the pain.

It was a few days later and mid-afternoon by the time Bob helped Emma into her apartment. As they entered, she put the blue plastic hospital bag by the door. The bag, she was told by the discharge nurse, had the clothes she wore on the night of her accident. Bob was holding a bag of groceries and her medications from their errand on the way home.

"I'll take care of this for you." Bob bent down and picked up the bag.

"No, thanks. I'll take care of it later." Emma took the bag from him, turned and opened the hall closet door and casually tossed the bag onto the floor of the closet before closing the door.

Emma looked around the long room that made up the living- and dining rooms. Nothing seemed to be hers. She didn't have any memories connected with her furniture, entertainment system or personal objects. In fact, it all seemed odd. Why? It quickly came to her—nothing seemed to be more than 10 years old.

"Any memories?"

Emma slowly shook her head 'no'. Pain immediately shot through her neck and to her bandaged forehead. She winced. "Why is there only one picture?" She went over to a single shelving unit and saw a picture of Bob and her smiling because they were on a ski vacation. Aspen. It was Aspen last year. She learned how to ski last year a month after she quit smok-'...

"You're not a 'picture-type' of person. I guess it's from being an only child."

"No. It's because of my mother. She died" *How do I know this?* "How did she die?"

"You were a Freshman in college."

"My father left us when I was 3." The memory of what her father looked like escaped her grasp.

"You said that when you're ready for pictures of your mother, you'll get them out. I guess you aren't ready yet." Bob shrugged. He really didn't want to talk about her mother.

"How did she die?" Emma now turned to Bob.

Bob thought about his answer. "Emma, do you want to know now?"

"Maybe later." Emma felt that her friend was trying to protect her. *But why no other photos?* She couldn't let the thought go.

"Do you want me to make dinner? I can make a mean bowl of tomato soup with crackers."

Emma allowed a very small smile escape in spite of the pain and a chance of making her lips bleed. "OK."

As promised, Bob made a bowl of soup for her. While she drank a cup of tea at the—her kitchen table, he cleaned up and did the dishes. They continued to talk about TV shows and entertainment news.

"I'll be back tomorrow afternoon if that's OK with you."

"That'll be good."

For the first week or so Bob came over everyday. After that, he came every other day and then once a week. He told her stories about their college days, parties they attended that were given by mutual friends, and last year's ski trip. All the stories Bob told her were just that, stories. None of the events were familiar to her.

It was during a ride to one of her doctor's appointments when Emma asked Bob about his family—and then she asked him about her mother's death.

"Emma." Bob hesitated. "Are you sure you want to know?"

"Yes. I think I do."

Bob began. "We were coming back to our floor after Biology. When our RA took you into the lounge. Took *us* into the lounge." He corrected himself. "You made me go with you." Bob quickly took his eyes from the street and gave Emma a fleeting, reassuring smile before looking back to his driving. He continued. Your mother took an overdose of pills. She was being treated for depression…" Bob quickly looked at Emma again to see if he should continue. "They found street drugs in her system too."

Nothing seemed to register with Emma. Bob could have read a passage out of a novel and she would still have the same feeling of detachment. "I don't remember." She didn't even remember her own mother. A spark. She did have one memory—she remembered a lady who liked to wear her hair in a single long braid.

* * *

Emma wasn't allowed to drive yet, so together Bob and she mapped out the public transportation system. The first day out

Emma took a trip to the art museum and got lost by taking the wrong connecting bus. Within a week she was navigating the bus and subway lines like a pro. She even memorized two bus routes.

After two months, she was allowed to return to work—if only part-time at first. Emma hoped the surroundings of her work place would jog her memory. She lied to her doctor that she was ready to return to work. In truth, she was terrified of returning to a job she didn't remember knowing how to perform and to a place that wasn't familiar to her. She couldn't even recall her work friends or fellow colleagues. Yet, she was bored at home and not having those memories made her angry with herself. In all of her fear and anger, Bob only came in the evenings after work—when he *did* visit and the conversations were dominated by his day at the office.

The night before returning to work, Emma looked for the blue plastic hospital bag. She remembered that she had moved it to the back of her bedroom closet. Where did she put it? She was getting frustrated with herself. Oh, that's right, she moved it again to her bathroom next to her clothes hamper. She went to her bathroom to look for it. Strange. She could have sworn she had put... Now she remembered! She was bored enough yesterday to wash her kitchen, hallway, and bathroom floors.

Emma was so happy that she was returning to work. She called Bob yesterday and told him her wonderful news.

"Great!" Was it her imagination? Or did he hesitate? Emma didn't want to believe so. "I'll tell Vince that you're coming back. I'll pick you up around 7:00—the usual time."

We carpooled? "Vince."

"Our boss."

"Hold on. We went to college together; we're friends; and we have the same boss?" This seemed so bizarre to her.

"Are you sure you're ready to come back to work?"

"I remember the office." She lied.

"I hope so. There's a ton of work I could give you. Don't worry. I'll do the presentation you were working on before...before your leave."

"Oh, yeah. I remember working on it." She lied again.

Emma's thoughts returned to the present task. She was kneeling on the floor of her bathroom. Emma opened the plastic blue bag and looked inside. She pulled out a pair of dirtied jeans. The pants, by the label and detail, weren't something one would find in a local discount chain store. Then she reached in and pulled out a blood-stained blouse. The once all white shirt seemed to be equally expensive just by the name on the label.

When Emma unfolded the shirt, something plopped in her lap. She looked down. It was a small white and silver evening clutch purse with silver trim. Wasn't the clutch part of a dream?

Emma picked up the clutch and opened it. Inside, there was a business issued ID, a credit card, a tube of lipstick, and a set of keys with a simple leather and jade charm key chain. There were also some coins and a few bills nestled in a pocket of the bag. Emma was more interested in the business ID then anything else. Why did she have her business ID with her and not her driver's license? Wasn't she in the hospital because of a car accident? She stared at her picture then at her name. Why did she feel that her ID wasn't real? Even the credit card seemed foreign to her. She placed her ID and credit card on the floor before picking up her keys. One key, by the emblem impressed onto it, was for a car that no longer existed because of the accident. (Emma felt lucky that Bob was handling everything with the insurance companies). The other keys were for the entrance to her building, mailbox, and her apartment's door. The last key, she suspected, was for her office.

She winced as her head began to hurt. She tried not to care about the oncoming pain. Instead, she held the keys tightly and left the clutch, and the remainder of its contents on her bathroom floor among the pile of soiled and damaged clothes and went to her hall closet. She found her satchel that she used for work. She rummaged through the large bag's pockets and found what she was looking for—a second set of keys. Except this set didn't have the key she assumed would be to her office.

Why?

What was she doing on the night of her accident that she was carrying the set of keys that had her office key and business ID in an evening bag?

She had the dream again that night.

* * *

She was wearing a very expensive white formal gown. She just finished fastening the ankle strap of her left shoe when her husband held open a velvet covered box from an exclusive jeweler to present Emma its contents.

"It's beautiful!" She held out her left wrist so that he could fasten the gold bracelet for her.

"I thought it would be a perfect match for the necklace I gave you last year."

"I always thought you had exceptional taste." Emma gave him a kiss. "Thank you. And by the way, you look great in a tuxedo."

She didn't see his face. She couldn't remember any of his facial features…the drone of the alarm clock woke her up.

* * *

Emma's weeks were filled with doing busy, unimportant work at the office. Wasn't it her imagination or was someone always babysitting her? She could have sworn that she overheard one of the secretaries talking to Vince about her.

It was yet another boring day of researching and paperwork. The day was June 28.

June 28.

She had a flash of a memory about her white and silver clutch. Maybe she was hiding something in it. Emma had put down the stack of papers on one of the filing cabinets and went back to her office for her satchel. She rooted around the bag until she found the little clutch that she now used as her money and coin purse. It was early for her to eat lunch; but she felt an impulse to look at the little bag more thoroughly—without one of her many babysitters watching her.

Emma almost ran for the elevator as Bob came darting out of his office after her. *Sorry, guy.* Emma was pleased with herself that she managed to escape.

She blended with the lunch-time crowd exiting the building from the lobby and walked five blocks in a new direction until she was standing in line at a sandwich shop that she thought she never visited before. She took her sub and small drink and sat down in a park.

She ate half her sandwich before she decided that this moment was good a time as any to examine her clutch. The purse was a little soiled now from constant use and the silver around the clasp was scratched. Emma snapped it open and felt around the lining. Nothing. She looked at the folded bills and coins. She took out her keys and examined them (perhaps for the 100th time). She even tried to peel apart the leather and jade decorative charm on the key ring. Nothing. Her business ID held no new clues to her past. Her state issued ID was a recent replacement for her driver's license. Her cell phone was a recent purchase to replace the one that she probably lost in the accident. She read the numbers on her credit card. Nothing.

Nothing.

Nothing.

Nothing.

Just a few things stuffed in a dirty silver and white clutch.

Dirty silver white clutch.

Silver white.

Silver white.

White gleam.

Gleam.

Gleaming.

She didn't know why, she had to cross the street. Emma quickly stuffed the contents of the purse back inside and threw away the remainder of her lunch. She dodged traffic and pedestrians. Now she was almost sprinting—heading two blocks east. She was acting on another impulse. Her feet stopped at a pawn shop. Emma didn't understand but she knew that something was important enough for her to go inside.

She allowed her eyes to adjust to the dim lighting. It didn't take a minute before she saw the jewelry in the jewelry display case. On the top shelf were her necklace and matching bracelet among some other pieces that she knew weren't hers.

There was a sudden flash of the memory of a bracelet being fastened on her wrist.

"You're back." A middle-aged man came around a corner of a rack of guitars. "I can't forget you. You've made a real impression. Are you going to pick up your stuff?"

"Yes. I want it all back."

"I already sold two of your necklaces and a pair of earrings."

"Whatever is left."

The man took out a receipt book and then the display boxes showing three bracelets, a zebra pin, and a gold and ruby necklace.

"I can't forget you. You made some impression." He said, as he put a bracelet, a necklace, and the pin in front of Emma.

"You already said that." She tried to read his expression. Was he trying to see if she would buy someone else's zebra pin? Emma immediately recognized the gold and ruby necklace and *the bracelet!* It was the gold bracelet with the heart-shaped charm!

By her expression, the man assessed his chances of overcharging Emma. A woman came out of a back room. Emma thought she was his wife. It was just three seconds. It was a chance and Emma took it: He turned to speak to the woman and then that's when Emma made an impulsive move. She grabbed the bracelet and ran out of the door. *It was her bracelet!* The couple tried to stop her but Emma moved too quickly and she disappeared into the lunchtime crowd of pedestrians.

Emma ducked into a coffee shop's bathroom. She examined her bracelet. She looked at the red impression the jewelry left in her hand because she held it so tightly in her fist. She read the inscription engraved on it: *Our Star Forever.*

A flash of memory—Gleaming… Star.

The company's new product had a gleaming star as it's logo.

FLASH! There were more flashes of memory.

Emma remembered

Standing next to her husband on the bottom of a ski slope. With Bob. And her husband's name was Bradley.

They were posing for a photo.

The ski attendant asked the threesome if they were ready for him to take the picture.

The photo in Emma's apartment wasn't real. Bradley's image was removed. The apartment wasn't really hers.

Another memory.

And another memory.

Bradley removed her driver's license from her clutch. It was her idea before…she had her…

No one would be looking for something as simple as a missing *key*.

Because

Because

Bradley and she were in the lab. The big gala was going to be held that night. It was Emma's idea that she would the one to be programmed by Synaptic Reflex Control. There would be several triggers, or rather *keys*, as Bradley called them. He removed her driver's license—that was the first (trigger) key. The second trigger to her memory was her business ID and set of office keys. The third memory trigger was the date, June 28. She wrote the program for the Synaptic Reflex Simulator for her to go to the pawn shop on June 28. The final trigger was the gold bracelet. If the bracelet was sold, then a sub-program would be initiated: She would remember the engraving on the charm.

They knew the truth. They knew. Emma put the bracelet in her clutch and started back to the office.

Emma walked through the lobby and towards the elevators when she passed a little girl and her mother. They were coming from the daycare that was in the building. Was it Emma's imagination or did the girl's eyes suddenly go white as they passed her? Emma wanted to shake the thought away but there was another memory...about children...

* * *

Emma was in one of the labs listening to 10 year-old Lisa Anne perform an aria perfectly. She looked to her fellow colleague, Michelle, and then at the voice coach who was accompanying Lisa Anne on piano. Emma returned her attention back to Subject No. 55836.

As noted in the extensive initial tests and interviews, Lisa Anne lived with her father and little sister, Rachel in the shelter across town. The three came to there six months ago. The father's comments in the reports showed that he felt it was better than having the girls placed in foster care.

He also commented how Lisa Anne and Rachel's mother spent almost eight years 'dating' other men off and on and then returning to the girls and him. Dad really believed that every time Mom returned it was for good. After all, Rachel's arrival three years ago was proof that it was for good. After Dad lost his job, Mom found someone else who was better and asked him for a divorce.

A few weeks after arriving at the shelter, Lisa Anne and Rachel were greeted by a man who was opening up a new daycare and after-school program: something new, exceptional, and free. Lisa

Anne was tested and she was one of seven children who were said to be 'special' by the people who came to visit the families in the evenings. All Dad had to do was sign some papers and let the daycare's teachers encourage her special and unique gifts to shine while he was out looking for work. As far as he was concerned, enrolling his girls in the daycare was the best decision of his life. After all, Lisa Anne was doing so well in school and was bringing home all A's and B's. Now she was able to sing like an angel.

After a few weeks in the program, the results were spectacular: three children were gifted musicians, two children were brilliant singers; one excelled in gymnastics, one showed promise in gymnastics and ballet, and two children were wonderful in painting and sculpting. All ten children showed exceptionally high intelligence. There was an added bonus—they could also read minds when they focused. However, that little detail was the teachers' and children's little secret.

Dr. Emma and her colleagues were serving the betterment of humankind. After all, the first recipients of this exceptional gift and discovery were the children of the poor, working-poor, and wards of the state. Just look at the miraculous results: the daycare seemed to churn out articulate, gifted, and intelligent geniuses. Someday very soon, all ten children were going to be the first in what was hoped to be many more to be a benefit to society.

The last notes on the piano echoed. Emma was so pleased; it was difficult to stop from applauding. "That was beautiful, Lisa Anne! Why don't you go to the study room and have a snack."

"Thanks, Dr. Emma." Lisa Anne showed a crooked-toothed

smile. Emma thought it was one of the first smiles since losing her mother and coming to the shelter. Lisa Anne seemed to wince. It was only a moment but Dr. Michelle saw it.

"Are you OK, Lisa Anne?" The girl nodded her head 'yes'.

The voice coach came over to join the two doctors as Lisa Anne left the room. "She's exceptional. I think she'll be ready to perform professionally within a year-and-a-half. I keep telling my husband how great this place is and he doesn't believe me."

Michelle smiled and feigned surprise. "Really? Do you think she'll be ready for next month's city-wide young performer's competition?"

"I think she could easily win the top award." She looked at her watch. "Please excuse me. I have another student." The voice coach gathered her music and bag by piano.

Emma waited until the door closed after the voice coach. "I just came from another session. From how he danced, I think two of our clients will have their pre-packaged creativity next year."

"And Bradley."

"From how well the children are developing their telepathy, our other client will have their product in two years."

"Lisa Anne was complaining about a headache today."

Emma reached into her jacket's left pocket for her ever-present tin of mints. "Increase her dose so she keeps her implants.

* * *

Emma had to focus. She tried to figure out a way of getting on to a computer without anyone finding out what she was up to.

She stepped out of the elevator and looked around the office to see who was still at lunch. Good—one cubicle showed its occupant's monitor still on with no password lock. Someone's sloppiness was her stroke of luck.

She walked in the room, sat down in front of the computer, and began to type. Her fingers seemed to have a mind of their own as they danced along the keys. It only took her a minute to find the answer after the company's logo blazed on the monitor. Emma saw schematics, photos, and even parts of logs. Her mind snapped to a million more memories. And children.

* * *

They were in her office.

"Emma, you got to read this." Bradley stuffed a memo into her hands. Her eyes quickly darted from word to word and paragraph to paragraph of the first two pages and then she flipped through the other nine pages.

"Sonufabitch. Three kids rejected the implants and we're going to take the blame if this gets out to the public. She fished into her jacket for her tin of mints. Damn it!! Empty! She pawed her other jacket pocket for a stick of gum.

"Emma…"

"And Vince is going to fire us the day after the Gala!"

"…We have…"

"It's our research! Our blood! Our life! ALL OF IT!" She was chomping on the gum as if it were a tough piece of meat.

"…There's something more important than being fired. Didn't you read the paragraph about?…"

"We lose all the rights! All the money! OUR FUTURE!"

"…It was more than implant rejection. Those children will never be the same."

"What are we supposed to do out it?" She threw the memo on her desk.

"We need to fix this."

* * *

Security would be here any moment because they would be alerted by

Emma was the real key.

Her mind would unlock everything that Bradley and she hidden.

It was the night of the company's gala. Her husband and their partner were going to announce their plans to market their breakthrough project: Synaptic Reflex Control. The Synaptic Reflex Simulator was going to cure the criminally insane by erasing the mind and then super imposing a healthy psyche. wouldn't it be wonderful to take the next step and expand and improve the human mind? Yet, it had one drawback: there was a chance it could also destroy the human mind as well. Bradley hid all the documentation on Synaptic Reflex Control in the system—making the data bounce from one company holding to the next without any one being able to retrieve it. Then he programmed Emma. If he couldn't stop the production by denouncing the project at the gala, then the program in Emma's mind would be triggered and her memory would be erased. Emma would be spared; because she was the key to finding all the documentation.

"I'm sorry you figured it out, Emma." She spun the chair around to see Bob looking at her. "We were hoping you wouldn't remember."

Two security guards walked up and stood behind Bob.

"Please come with us, Doctor," said one of the guards. Emma slowly stood and was lead down the hall by the three men.

"You're a bastard," she spat at Bob.

"No. I'm a visionary like you."

Synapse

Synapse: The point of junction between two neurons in a neural pathway. The impulse traveling in the first neuron initiates an impulse in the second neuron. They are susceptible to fatigue, offer a resistance to the passage of impulses, and are markedly susceptible to the effects of oxygen deficiency, anesthetics, and other agents, including therapeutic drugs, toxic chemicals, and Synaptic Reflex Control (SRC) under the Synaptic Reflex Test (SRT)."

* * *

The newly hired technician looked at the woman in the next room through the glass window. The medicine was starting to take hold. She wouldn't mind the Test so much. The tech concentrated on looking at all the leads he had place on her. It was better that he thought the leads. He didn't want to look at the "Dream Machine." He didn't want to think about the "Dream Machine" and the Test. He didn't want to think about the leads that were attached to her head, chest, and arms, or that the leads connected her to the "Dream Machine's" monitors. When was the doctor going to come in? When could he start the Test and have it be done with? Why was everything so white and plain?

The technician stopped himself. He looked at his blank monitor and then at the other blank monitor which was for the attending doctor. Everything the woman in the "Dream Machine" would hear and see; they would hear and see a voyeuristic moment later on the upper half of their monitors in viewing format and in program format on the lower half of their monitors.

The doctor came in and sat down in front of the other monitor. She opened up the chart she was carrying. She asked the tech to start the Test.

The technician started keying in the initial commands on his keyboard.

Click. Click-click-click. Clink, click. Click. Click.

The Candidate in the other room could hear someone typing on a keyboard. It must be the leads near her ears. Who cares. Maybe she did. But, why couldn't she see anything? Everything was black.

Click-click. Click. Click. Click, click-click.

The doctor saw black on the upper half of her monitor. She looked at the lower half of the monitor to see what data the technician was inputting and the corresponding running program.

Click-click, click. Click-click. Click. Click, click-click.

The technician glanced at the upper half of his monitor. It was still black. He looked back down at the lower half. Data input and the Test's program were scrolling. Now the lower half of his monitor read

LEVEL ONE NOW BEGINNING

The Candidate saw black. The doctor and technician still saw the upper half of their monitor glare black. Click. Click.

Then the Candidate saw gray. The doctor and technician saw their monitor flick to a gray patch.

The technician continued to type as the program progressed.

The monitors flicked gray.

Then gray again.

Randa walked up to the doors of the "Yellow Bird." She glanced at her reflection in the black glass doors. When was the last time she wore a dress? Seventh grade? That was the time when she was cat-called Randolph and residual matter was called something else.

The lower half of the technician's monitor read

RESIDUAL MATTER

Miranda had to sing tonight in her 7th grade chorus for the annual open house for Pullman Middle school. He mother had worked two extra shifts cleaning the building at 700 East to buy the customary "ribbony" dress. Miranda couldn't bear to tell her mother that she thought the dress was unbelievably ugly. The thing was yellow and it had yards and yards of ribbons and ruffles. She felt like an old lady's parlor curtain she saw once in an old movie. Because there was so little money (for a lack of a better way to say poverty-stricken), her mother couldn't afford new shoes for her. So, Miranda wore her old street shoes to the open house. Miranda felt extremely self-conscience and awkward in that hideous dress and her raggedy shoes. She knew she would stand out among some of her classmates: the rich-daddy's-girl-types. She forced herself to walk into her homeroom where she and the other 7th graders would wait to line up and go on stage. Everyone would see her: the proverbial disadvantaged ugly duckling permitted through the city's funding and good humor to attend a school for the privileged.

The room seemed so surreal. The old fashioned city surplus fluorescent lights cast an unfriendly light and the windows showed black reflections. To Miranda, the room seemed harsh and cruel.

Jeannie Houghton glanced in Miranda's way and stopped talking among her circle of friends. She whispered something in the ear of her friend to her right. Miranda tried not to notice this as she made her way to her desk. On her way to school with her mother, aunts, and uncles, she had hoped that Jeannie (who was the richest and most popular of the richest and popular) would leave her alone—or had been hit by a bus on the way to school tonight. But no, Jeannie, the leader of the elite-pack had made the orders to surround Miranda like vultures. Miranda wished her friends from her neighborhood were here. Miranda pulled out her history book and started to read. She tried at least ignore the audible whispering, sniggering and giggling that seemed to fly in a circle around her.

One of the 8th grade teachers entered the room and told the class to line up to go on stage. The class did so: tall boys lined up first, then short boys, tall girls third, and short girls last. Miranda was in the middle. Jeannie and some of her friends were directly behind Miranda.

She heard fresh waves of giggling. Miranda wished she could stop Jeannie and her giggle-fest friends from teasing her. But she couldn't. Her family would be disappointed in her and she would probably be beaten by her mother, then her father (when he came to visit), and each of her relatives in turn if they learned she was suspended, or worse, expelled because of a fight on the night of the school's annual open house.

One of Jeannie's friends called out from behind Miranda. "Hey, Randolph! Boys don't wear dresses!"

Miranda heard another one of Jeannie's friends add, "I bet Randolph's wearing a bra, too!"

"What for?" Jeannie giggled.

Miranda felt the tug and snap at her back. She tried to shrug them off and give them dirty, tough looks. It didn't help when she turned back around to face the doorway.

Snap. Snap. Snap.

She couldn't fight back. She was always reminded that they were better than she. Her mother told her the only way she could prove that she was their equal was if she graduated among them. She couldn't fight back. If she did, a teacher would come in and she would get the blame. Her kind always did. Besides, her whole family was out in the audience. So, let her classmates think what they wanted about her and maybe Miranda's friends and she would get chance to...

Snap. Snap. Snap. What if she could forget about giving the girls tough looks and punch them instead? A real fight.

The monitors saw

Gray
Gray

RESIDUAL MATTER

It was the next day after PE. They were in the locker room and the same girls tried an encore performance of the night before.

Snap. Snap. Snap. SNAP.

No more. No more bra snapping. No more lunches spilled on purpose. No more teasing, giggling, or spit wads during study period. No more!

Something in Miranda pulled and tore. She grabbed Jeannie. Miranda bounced her against the lockers so hard that the old and worn locks jiggled. Jeannie looked too surprised to defend herself. Somewhere in her exhilaration, Miranda felt a spreading hush come over the room. She knew the other girls had stopped in mid-change to listen for the direction of where the noise was coming from. Miranda didn't care about the other girls. Miranda was too occupied in the shear pleasure of the resound of locks and body made against metal lockers. She liked it so much, in fact, that Miranda continued to bounce Jeannie some more.

Body against metal. Humphff. Body against metal. Humphff. Again and again. Miranda really liked the rhythm of it.

By now the whole room was jammed into the one corner. Girls were trying to get a glimpse of the fight. A popular girl was getting beaten up by an unpopular girl. There goes the theory of "popular relativity" shot to hell.

Miranda was angry and exhilarated at the same time. She was more angry than anything else. She took her anger out on Jeannie. Miranda punched Jeannie just to emphasize how she felt. The girl crumpled to the cement floor in a sobbing, blubbering, bruised (and, yes) very humbled pile of person.

Miranda realized something. What? She didn't have to be the person they wanted her to be.

Miranda turned to the other girls who were screaming at her. Yet, Miranda realized, no one came to Jeannie's defense. Miranda thought everything over as she was lead down to her counselor's office by her PE teacher. No one helped Jeannie. Miranda could bet that her friends would have helped her if the situation was reversed. Maybe that was way Jeannie and her friends made sure Miranda was alone.

RESIDUAL MATTER

Miranda was not expelled: It seemed the school needed the city's funding. She was given a three day suspension and five detentions. When her parents found out, her father beat her. Her mother told her now disappointed she was of her daughter. Her mother's disappointment had hurt Miranda more than the beating.

RESIDUAL MATTER

She was in the counselor's office. Again. This time it was for trying to decorate the halls with one of Jeannie's friends. Being in trouble was OK, fine, and great. She didn't start the fights. It was bad being punished when she got home. At least she got into less fights now that Jeannie and her friends finally learned to avoid her. The boys thought it was a regular laugh that one person could do so much damage to popularity, esteem, and the American way of the private school system.

Their monitors showed

END OF RESIDUAL MATTER

The Candidate in the "Dream Machine" heard somewhere in the far distance a familiar noise.

Perhaps computer keys were being clicked.

The technician continued to type data into the program to pull the Candidate back in:

Now she wore an expensive designer business suit. Her feet were screaming with pain. The high heeled shoes she wore felt like vices that should have never been started in the first place.

The person who thought up high heels for women must have been an Oedipal sadist. But, her outfit was just for show, as being known as the owner of the "Yellow Bird Night Club."

* * *

The technician looked over to his left to see the doctor make some notes in the Candidate's chart.

"Please end Level One and begin Level Two."

"Yes, Doctor."

Data input for Level Two began.

The monitors showed

LEVEL TWO NOW BEGINNING

The Candidate felt tugging on the sides of her head. She saw

Gray

Gray

* * *

Memories. That was what

RESIDUAL MATTER

was called.

She was a junior in high school. "Miranda" was slurred to "Randy". She liked to walk around the school halls in her socks. The boys mistook this habit of comfort as sensual. Sensual meant sexy and sexy was a sure thing on a date. She was on her first real date. Her date took her to an abandon warehouse where just about everyone from high school partied. He was all over Randa like a back ally dog. He was just trying to have some fun at her expense. For his efforts of affection, he ended up in a lot of pain. She was a pretty good street fighter and very lucky.

RESIDUAL MATTER

After high school graduation, the family's neighbor, a retired cop in 5F encouraged her to apply to the Academy. She was accepted. Local girl makes good.

Gray
Gray

RESIDUAL MATTER

She was walking down the hall from the rec. room. She was at the City's Police Academy. She had a copy of her application and she just finished talking to one of her friends.

She wanted to review her application. She was called "Randa" now. The "boys" at the Academy thought Randy was someone who was a poster pin-up girl wearing only skimpy clothes. They mistook her as someone that would be found on the beach with her best friends: Brandie, Candi, and A-leading-brand-of-Suntan-lotion-with-coconut-scent.

She was near the elevators. She saw some of the "boys" get on. One stuck his head out and she could hear suppressed laughing (snickering). On, no, the dreaded "Favorite Prank" and here comes the "Favorite Prankee" padding down the hallway in her socks. OK, here we go, people.

She stepped on the elevator, pressed the lighted "7" and stepped and quickly slid to the side of the elevator.

Someone enthusiastically yelled, "Lights out!"

It became black. One moron had even disconnected the emergency light.

Randa made sure she her back was against the elevator wall. She heard shuffling and yells as she quickly inched her way to the open control panel. She flipped the light back on and then closed the control panel. What everyone on the elevator saw was a pathetic and lonely man's dream gone amuck. They looked like a bunch of horny men holding on to each other's asses. Yes, folks, another game of "can-you-grab-her-ass-before-we-get-to-the-next-floor". Or, better know as the "Favorite Prank".

"Having fun, boys?" She said in her best "Randa-come-hither-voice". The doors opened and she stepped out on the 7th floor.

She turned around just to get a good look at the stupid expressions on their faces. She went to her dorm room, closed the door, and laughed.

Gray

RESIDUAL MATTER

She was laughing in the judge's chambers. Not because it was funny. Far from the truth. It was a nervous laughter and laughing kept her from killing someone.

"You've got to the kidding me?"

"This is the best offer." Randa's lawyer looked very serious.

She gave a single dry cough-laugh and a half smile. "I'd rather take my chances in jail."

"You know you won't last a day there. You're a know cop."

Now she erupted. It was a real rage. "Look, dog puke, I didn't do it! And!" She roared in his face. "I get some piss poor, snot nosed, candy-ass lawyer telling me that if I become a Courier, everything will work out OK! Either way I'm dead. And what makes you so sure I won't sell out?!"

A guard grabbed her shoulders and threw her back into her chair. Randa pushed his hands away from her. She tried to calm down.

The judged cleared his throat before speaking. "If you decide to become a Courier, we will give you a new identity and relocate you. To a much better residence. In fact, all Couriers tend to have a better life. Provided they do not illegally upload."

"What if I do? After all, I'm an ex-cop!" she yelled at the lawyer. She looked at the judge again. "And con now."

END OF RESIDUAL MATTER

* * *

"Please begin Level Three," the doctor said. The doctor wrote in the Candidate's chart that the Core Program of the SRT was now beginning.

"Beginning Level Three now."

Randa heard the clicking of the technician's computer keys in the far distance.

Click. Click-click-click-click, click, click. Click.

click

Their monitors showed

LEVEL THREE NOW BEGINNING

Randa felt tugging at the sides of her head. She saw

Gray
Gray

The monitors showed

Gray
Gray

And then

Black

Let the Test (games) begin.

* * *

The technician was typing in date input:

"Randa," her partner whispered over the bar. He was disguised as a bartender. "You ready?"

"Don't worry about me," she whispered back as she glanced towards the stage. She said more audibly, "Phil, give me my usual."

"Yes, Ma'am." A new band was playing. She liked them. They were good. Too bad for them.

"The one on guitar." Phil whispered.

"I know," she whispered back. She said in a louder tone, "Hold that drink will yeah?" She walked away from the bar and towards the stage.

The bad stopped when they saw her walking over to them.

"Don't stop on my account. I like what I'm hearing."

The guitar player looked down to her from the stage. "And who's hearing it?"

"The owner of the 'The Yellow Bird'. That makes me your boss, now doesn't it?" Guitar Player and his band became edgy. She gave each other nervous glances. Good. She enjoyed intimidating people. "Don't worry, I won't fire you. Yet."

"I'm real sorry," Guitar Player said.

"Good. Then to apologize, you can come to my place tonight,

say eight o'clock. Meet some of my friends, have a few drinks, and sign a contract. Get the directions from that guy behind bar." She turned around and walked away. Then she stopped and pivoted so that she could turn her head to the band. She liked this movement and stance. She called it her 'Randa Move' from her Academy days. She thought it made people uneasy and therefore easy to control. "If you're going to be late, then forget it." She turned and continued walking. She went past the bar.

"Bye, Ms. Mansfield."

"See yeah, Phil."

Randa felt tugging.

See-yeah-Phil. See-yeah-Phil.

She saw

Gray

Somewhere in the distance computer keys clicked.

Randa saw the "Yellow Bird" change to white stone and black wrought iron fence and

Black

Gray

Gray

Her chauffeured car drove up the driveway, past the electronic security system, and into the car port. She left herself out and walked into the east entrance way of her mansion.

"They're in the living room." She gave Diane, a fellow officer, her jacket and purse. Diane was dressed as a maid.

"Thanks." Randa walked down the hallway and into the sunken living room—a remnant of the 1970s and '80s. She looked around and saw two of the band members. One of them was Guitar Player. A couple, named John and Mary, was sitting on the long sofa. Randa knew that John and Mary were somehow part of the Test: decoys and decoration. Her fiance and fellow officer, Mike, was sitting in a chair next to John and Mary. Mike was undercover as a business man. She sat down in a chair that was next to Mary.

John got up and went over to Randa.

"May I get you anything?"

"Just a tonic, John." John went across the room to the bar.

Randa announced to her guests, "Well, I'm sorry I'm late. But, I had a business meeting." John walked back to Randa and handed her a glass with ice and tonic before he returned to his seat. "Thanks."

Mary smiled at Randa. "How was your dinner?"

"You know me too well. It was fine." She took a sip from her glass. "I think we should talk about their contract." She said looking at the two musicians. "Don't you, Mike?"

"I have it right here." He walked over the bar and opened his briefcase to get the band's contract and a pen. As he walked over to Guitar Player, he clicked the pen. Mike held out the contract and pen for Guitar Player. Guitar Player took the contract without looking up at Mike and started to read the first page.

"We've already discussed it, so I hope you understand the terms of the deal. If so, then just sign." Still not looking at Mike, Guitar Player took the pen and scrawled his name on the contract before passing the paperwork and pen to his band mate.

"Welcome to the 'Yellow Bird', gentlemen," Randa said.

Somewhere computer keys clicked: more data input and another tug at the sides of her head.

Gray

Guitar Player's band mate handed Mike the contract and the pen. Randa could tell how hungry the two were. They had that look that desperate, expectant people have when they are on the edge of something. She had that same look (a long time ago).

Computer keys clicking...

Gray
Gray
Black

LEVEL FOUR NOW BEGINNING

Randa saw the room in dimmed lights. She was still in her seat. She saw Mike dead, the couple and the other band member gone. Oh, God, no, please no. Mike!

Guitar Player was standing over her with a gun.

"Let's go to the 'Yellow Bird'."

Randa would show no fear. No, not to this pile of low life.

"My keys are in my purse." Her gun was in her purse.

"Don't worry about your car. We'll use mine. And..." Guitar Player gave a wry smile. "Your lawyer boyfriend gave me his key to the Club."

Randa walked up the stairs of the living room with Guitar Player behind her. She thought

of

RESIDUAL MATTER

the degradation she had to go through as a girl. She thought of the Bra Snappers. Snap. Snap. Snap.

END OF RESIDUAL MATTER

She pivoted, kicked, and jammed him in the neck. Getting the gun was unbelievably simple after that movement. Guitar Player was a writhing heap of pain. Randa wanted to shoot him to help him in his painful moment. No more wealthy women to kill and then rape. Some signature, Pal. Should've stayed with the music. Had a real talent there.

Computer keys. Click. Click, click. Click-click-click...

Randa smelled something old and familiar. Something that was from her childhood. Gas. She smelled gas. And she was going to fire a gun! She put the safety on.

She looked down at the writhing man on the floor again. He

stopped writhing when the butt of his gun struck the side of his head.

Click-click-click-click. Click, Click. Click. Click.

Where's Diane. And the others?

LEVEL FIVE NOW BEGINNING

Gray

Gray

She ran towards the kitchen. Randa found Diane in the hallway, on the hallway, and in the dining room. She wouldn't get sick. Randa clutched the gun for some obscure comfort. She would think of

RESIDUAL MATTER

The Bra Snappers.

END OF RESIDUAL MATTER

She got to the kitchen. John and Mary were tied and gagged in chairs. Band Player looked deranged: the kind of look that could glaze over the eyes and make the mind do anything— unexpectedly. He was holding the couple at gun point. Somewhere in Randa's mind she wanted to kill. It was a good thing the safety was on the gun. Randa couldn't help herself when she saw the absurdity in this situation. She didn't feel like going up in one huge fireball because of him.

"I *would* like to kill them." That look was the only thing that stopped Randa from laughing at the fool. And his gun. At least John and Mary were not in between Band Player and her.

"OK. Here." Randa tossed him her gun. She did the same thing to him as she did to Guitar Player. Not really. She used Band Player's head to break the kitchen door's window to let in fresh air.

She untied her two friends. Next on the agenda, fellow board members, is to call the cops—and vomit when we think of Mike and Diane. Right now, we should think of how lucky we are that Band Player's gun didn't go off.

Click. Click. Click-click-click.

* * *

Randa heard a doctor say something somewhere to a tech. Where? "Please bring her up."

"Yes, Doctor. Bringing her up now."

Click. Click. Click, click, click, click. Click-Click.

Gray

Gray

Gray

Black

Black

"You did very well for your first time, Randa." The doctor still seemed so far away. "However, you had put your friend and fiance in your Test. That's a high emotional factor. you also remembered stressful childhood experiences. I'm afraid we'll need to erase memories of people and places during further testing. Once we are satisfied that you are free of 'incompatible residual matter' we can give you the implants. As we explained before, the implants are necessary. They'll give you a new life as a Courier."

Computer keys. Click. Click-click-click. Click, click.

Black

Black

"You're coming up. You're no longer under the Test." Randa heard the technician say to her.

Click. Click. Click. Click. Click-click. Click-click.

Black

Black

RECORDED MESSAGE

"Synaptic Reflex Test (Type 2). Sponsored by the City and ImagiNation, Inc. SRT (Type 2) can examine, under simulation, the ability of the Courier-in-training in potentially dangerous and ethically compromising situations..."

Randa felt another pull behind her eyes.

"Your SRT showed 40% residual matter, a rating of HIGH, synapse reflex showed HIGH. Emotional reaction showed 50%, a rating of AVERAGE. SRT is now complete.

END OF RECORDED MESSAGE

Gray
Gray

"The nest SRT will be a little more challenging, Randa. I think we'll give you five more SRTs. You need an emotional rating of 5% before we can give you the implants." The doctor's voice seemed closer to Randa now.

The doctor continued, "I think you were told about the implants, Randa. But, let's go through it again: The implants are extremely sensitive. For example, you choose to do something (anything in fact) illegal, such as you sell the information you're carrying to a competitor. When you upload that information, the implants will be triggered to cause a serious stroke in you.

Gray
Gray

Then the monitors flicked to

White

Residual Matter. Memories were called residual matter when she was in the 7th grade.

And the implants were going to help her to become part of the new System.

The Candidate opened her eyes.